About The Author

Miller Caldwell is a Scottish-based novelist. He graduated from London University having studied African industrial development, traditional African religions and the colonial history of West Africa. He has had articles published in health magazines and The Scottish Review.

In a life of humanitarian work in Ghana, Pakistan and Scotland, he has gained remarkable insights into human nature. He brought an African President to tears in West Africa in 2000 and he confronted Osama bin Laden in Abbottabad in 2006. He retired from being the Regional reporter to the children's hearings as he had mild cognitive impairment. He was, for twelve years, the local chair of the Scottish Association for The Study of Offending. He also served on the committee of the Society of Authors in Scotland, as its events manager

Miller plays a variety of brass, woodwind and keyboard instruments. This is mentioned because they provide a break from writing. Married, he has two daughters and lives in Dumfries.

A
LINGERING
CRIME

A novella about the hidden
evidence of sexual abuse

Miller H Caldwell

Matador
9 Priory Business Park,
Wistow Road, Kibworth Beauchamp,
Leicestershire. LE8 0RX
Tel: 0116 279 2299
Email: books@troubador.co.uk
Web: www.troubador.co.uk/matador
Twitter: @matadorbooks

ISBN 978 1789014 150

British Library Cataloguing in Publication Data.
A catalogue record for this book is available from the British Library.

Printed and bound by CPI Group (UK) Ltd, Croydon, CR0 4YY
Typeset in 12pt Adobe Jenson Pro by Troubador Publishing Ltd, Leicester, UK

Matador is an imprint of Troubador Publishing Ltd

This novel is dedicated to David and Jo
Benrexi.
A friend for almost five decades, David
travelled the route from Judaism to
Christianity clinging on to his trusty guitar
which shares his life with Jo. Through the
medium of YouTube, Facebook and e-mail
the Atlantic evaporates and I see and hear
David regularly playing and singing.
What a wonderful way to keep in touch
with dear friends in South Carolina while I
remain in Dumfries.

Acknowledgements

I must thank my cover designers at Spiffing Covers for that will be your first sight of this novella. Thank you Dr Debra D. Drown. You inspired this book. Many thanks too to Police Scotland at Dumfries, who clarified my thoughts and advised me of the criminal timeline. To David Benrexi for providing the American legal terms and jargon. Special thanks are due to David Watt former AFNOR translator, reviser and proof-reader who edited the script. But above all thanks and love are due to my wife Jocelyn, who gives me enough time to daydream, plot and write.

Contents

As some day it may happen that a victim may be found,
I've got a little list. I've got a little list.
Of society offenders who might well be underground,
and who never would be missed and who never would be missed.

Sir W.S. Gilbert. From The Mikado.

Author's Note

This novella is more than a story. It should be of interest to the judiciary in many lands. Judges, Sheriffs, Procurators Fiscal, defence solicitors, Crown Office Prosecutors and those engaged in the care and protection of victims. It is also a crime novel for those who enjoy that genre.

1

I WAS IN MY GARDEN ON MY KNEES WHEN I WAS arrested. I had been planting sweet peas in the last week of April, gambling on the end of winter frosts. I had already planted the first of two boxes. I heard a siren. I paid little attention to it. I always found it difficult to differentiate between alarm tones that I often heard from the busy road. Was it an ambulance this time or fire engine perhaps? No. The police car slowed down and entered the drive. I looked up. It was surely not coming for me? I confidently knew I had a guilt-free conscience though my face must have shown a degree of concern. The siren fell silent. I watched as the luminous car stopped in front of me. Two uniformed officers got out. I could not detect any friendly smile from either of them. Their stare fixed on mine. They approached me and took hold of my wrists. They gave the statutory patter of 'I must warn you anything which...' at such speed, I couldn't take it all in. You can't at the point of arrest.

The cuffs were on, behind my back, before I could contemplate what was happening. I straightened myself then stood with their assistance. I didn't know where to start as I felt my heart run away with itself.

They mentioned a man named McGraw, Daniel McGraw. It meant nothing. I thought they said Florida yet neither place nor person rang true for me.

'You must have the wrong guy. I haven't committed a crime,' I insisted as I was led, with hesitancy, to the police car.

'I've never heard of the victim and I've never been to Florida. You've got your cases mixed up, haven't you? I mean, a traffic offence, speeding maybe? Overstaying my parking time? Wrong Watson perhaps? Yes maybe I accept that...'

The officer put his hand on my head as I was lowered into the back seat of the police car. 'No sir. I told you... Murder. On February 23rd in Taylor County, Florida, you did murder Daniel McGraw.'

A shudder went through my body. Yes, I had heard right the first time. It left my fingers twitching behind my back. 'Christ, there's something far wrong here,' I said shaking my head side to side.

Me, Jack Watson, a widower, a man of sixty-five years of age, a writer, silver haired, spectacled and a pound or two over weight. God, what a mess I was in. But a murderer? No way.

'For God's sake, I assure you I've never even thought about murder. I couldn't. I've no motive. What's more I've never been in Florida. Georgia yes, in fact I flew back on the 25th but Florida? Some corpse you got there.'

I felt good I had got that out of my system.

'You'll be advised in due course,' the leaner of the two cops said.

'You guys are stubborn.' I hoped to provoke more information. I was wasting my breath. These uniformed servants were not your lollipop crossing supervisors. Serious crime, big fellas they were. They were not open to dialogue. Not a glimmer of doubt about the charge could I detect in the eyes of either officer.

Familiar streets sped by as we approached the police station. I kept my head low. Could I be seen behind the tinted glass? Would I be out by Thursday? I rarely missed my over 60s badminton games on that night. What would my friends think when they heard I was detained on a murder charge? An offence I knew I did not commit. The cell was stark save for some foul graffiti words and a drooping phallic drawing on the walls. A blue plastic mattress lay sloppily on a concrete bed. A fragrant smell surprised me. Some sort of sweat remover I suppose. There was an almost clinical atmosphere. The wards were however cells.

Open windows were not a feature. It wasn't a normal loo either. The U-bend went straight out of the wall and through some filter arrangement, apparently to trap drugs. What a job. It must be a police rookie that gets that one. They'll find only Werther's Originals in me. Loo paper had to be requested, I'm told. It seems if soaked, it can stick to the silent eye on the ceiling, watching my every move. To hell with them, I thought as I raised an inappropriate finger to express my bewilderment and anger.

'Hey anyone there?' I clung to the door window bars and turned my ear to the corridor. There was no answer. A feeling of conspiracy grew. I waited a few minutes.

'I said… is anyone there? Am I alone in this cage?' An older policeman approached my cell. A man who'd seen every type of criminal before, many times I assumed. He wandered through from his desk taking his time. He stopped his chewing. 'Yes? What do you want?' I spoke to him in a controlled voice. 'I want to know what this is all about. I want to get out and… well… sort these two wishes and I'll be satisfied.'

He shook his head with one hand on his left hip adjusting his trousers. 'Can't see you getting out. Murder is a serious offence, sir.'

I stuffed my hands into my pockets and nodded. 'I could not agree more but shouldn't I be told what I'm alleged to have done? Who is it I murdered? How come in Florida? When's my first court appearance? Come on, some answers please.'

The pleadings of an older man softened his response for a brief moment.

'Don't think a date is set for you yet sir.'

I could not believe what I was hearing. 'Well officer, it damn well should be. Habeas corpus and all that. Innocent till proved guilty. Heard of it?' I said raising my voice. He stood tall and threatening. 'Hey don't get wordy with me, sir. I'm here to make sure you are treated well. All I'm saying is it's a complicated case I've been told.'

Complicated, perhaps that meant identification doubts. It seemed an insignificant problem to me.

'What… complicated? You never had a murder case before?'

'Sure have. It's not just murder. It's beyond me really. The boss is working with the Crown Office. They'll make a decision soon. Maybe it will be your lucky day and the evidence will fall short. Anyway you'll get to meet the duty solicitor when he arrives. That's your right. He'll help you out.'

I sat down. Facts and problems flashed though my mind in an unordinary manner. My memory had failed me so very often over the past few years but with this charge I could not fault my mind's determined enquiry. It was sharp and on edge. A lump in my throat tightened. It stemmed from the apparently insignificant fact that I'd be separated from my accordion. That instrument had been with me since I was fourteen. It was my comforter then and still was today. It had shared my youthful anxieties, my confusion and my fears. To live without it left a hole in my heart. It had begun its life at the depth of my nightmare. I felt its missing keenly. It helped to keep me afloat. I cringed at the thought I'd never see it again.

Then lights brightened my mind all of a sudden. My song writing and my novels could be inspired by my situation. If only I had a pen and paper. That was currently denied. However they could not take the tunes from my head as long as I retained them. Yes, retained them. I needed them to calm me right now.

Shortly after 10 p.m. I was led along the wet disinfectant corridor floor. My nose wrinkled at its sharp odour. I caught a sniff of a cigarette smoke trail as I passed one fellow resident. He looked up and we exchanged a camaraderie lip-curved smile. We said nothing but wondered what brought each of us to this point in our lives.

I was led to the interview room within the detention suite. I waited, seated on a chair before a desk. Both items of furniture were chained to a small stone mound, cemented into the floor. Then I heard the click of stiletto heels approach. I was on edge. I had not expected to hear that.

'Mind your step, lass. The flair's wet,' said the officer in an almost patronising manner. The young female face peered round the door. It was fresh, virginal and bright eyed, optimistic perhaps. She had dressed for this occasion that was sure. A dark blue two piece suit and it looked new. It matched her tottering blue shoes giving her extra height. It was Saturday night and I was her date.

'In you go, dearie, he'll nae bite,' invited the policeman assigned and required by law to be within a reasonable distance from the interview room without hearing. It was a distance interpreted by considerable liberty each time, dependant on the accused's risk factor. I heard his footsteps fade. That told me something.

'Good evening, I'm your duty solicitor. You are Jack Watson?' she asked as I felt her eyes assess me, her client.

'Indeed. Do have a seat. Now you have an advantage over me. What's your name?' I asked to set the rules.

The solicitor momentarily hesitated. She seemed unsure whether she could tell me or perhaps I had forced my question too robustly.

'Listen, you have nothing to worry about meeting me. I did not commit murder. That's all you need to know.'

She smiled. Had I broken her reserved approach?

'New to this situation are you?' I asked in as supportive a manner as I could muster. My question disarmed her. She seemed to relax.

'No, not entirely new. No, third time actually. Breaches of the Peace and assaults mainly, so far.' She seemed to be gaining in confidence.

'First murder case then?' I asked with a disarming smile.

She nodded. Her cards had been played. We knew what each other had to know.

'Listen, there's always a first time for everything, except murder, of course.' I found myself grinning, holding back an earned laugh. I longed to put a comforting arm around her. My joke seemed to have fulfilled that purpose. She got underway.

'I'm Debbie Kelly. I graduated last year. I'm in my third month with Coyle & Patterson. Yes, first alleged murder case, as you rightly deduced.'

I gave a paternal smile. I liked to hear her say the word *alleged*. It gave me some hope.

'There are a few questions I must ask you.' She looked at her folder, as a set of bullet point questions came into view.

'How long have you been in custody?'

A simple question although it took a moment to think. 'Picked up mid afternoon on Friday and... er... this is Saturday night, right?'

She nodded and penned my reply diligently.

'Have you been given your meals?' she asked looking up at me.

'Yes, huh. Local takeaways they give me. I can't live this way without my vitamins. No fruit either.'

She merely ticked a box. 'Are you on any proscribed medication?' she asked.

'Lamotrigine, Amlodipine, Warfarin, and Nowamin -side.'

She smiled at my attempt at further humour. No wonder she asked the next question.

'Have you been given your medication?'

'Yup. Police doctor dropped them off at the desk and I've been given them at the right time.' I noticed her pen slip down the list. We were making progress.

'Does anyone know you are here?'

That changed my tune and she watched my smile evaporate. 'No, not till the papers tell them. I'm a widower.'

She lowered her voice out of respect.

'Have you been officially charged?'

'Yes, I have. God yes. It doesn't make sense at all. I don't know the victim; I've never been to the murder scene...'

She knew this was neither the time nor place to discuss evidence. She noted my response in great detail. There was a hesitation. A shuffling of feet came from the corridor then they faded away.

'Have you been offered the opportun...'

Her mid-sentence stopped unexpectedly. I could tell where she was heading. Opportunity indeed. A light bulb lit up my face.

'Perhaps you are asking whether I have been offered the opportunity to contact my lawyer. I have none. So, I think we can take that as a no but the process is well underway with you.'

She placed her pen between her lips. It hid her smile. I smiled. My instinct had been right.

'I have just one message to make clear. I don't know the man I am alleged to have murdered and I've never been anywhere near the site of this crime. I'll damn well repeat that till everyone hears. It's as simple as that.' My last sentence was long drawn out for effect.

'I have noted your clear denial, Mr Watson. I suppose there's not much that can be done till Monday. Even then, it's a very serious charge. I can't see you being released right away.' Her eyes looked up for a reaction.

'Monday's another day. As long as you tell an older colleague that I'll be at court on Monday morning. With respect, I need a senior partner to take on my murder charge. No offence. I hope this is a learning curve worth experiencing nevertheless.'

She nodded. Her smile was more relaxed this time.

'You have been very honest and helpful to me. I do appreciate what you have said and I have noted and underlined your clear denial of this offence. I'd say I would have thought the date, charge and locus should have been examined more carefully. I'll tell my colleagues of this apparent discrepancy.'

'Then I guess the interview is over. I've enjoyed it.' I felt it in all honesty, while at the same time recognising it to have been a necessary inconvenience. It seemed to take my case no further forward.

'I wish you well and if it's a case of mistaken identity or there is no evidence forthcoming, then I expect you to be out soon.'

I nodded. She bent down to gather her case.

She arose and had difficulty pushing her chair towards the table. She looked underneath and saw the anchored chain. We both laughed. Before the mirth faded, a policeman arrived and opened the door to let Miss Kelly out.

'Back to your cell, Mr Watson,' he growled.

I spent the rest of the weekend in the stark cell. No one else visited. My wife Joan died of breast cancer five years ago. God, what would she have made of this? God, are you letting her watch me now, silently from above? I hoped not. How I missed her terribly. No one would find me gone for some time, not until the press got hold of the story and what a story it would make. Not just murder, I remembered he said. I reflected on what the officer might mean. Murder with fraud? Murder with assaults? Mass murder? Too many questions and not enough answers to diminish the stress mounting in my head like an overheated car engine. I cursed my failing memory but still no explanation was emerging.

'When did I do it?' I uttered to the walls. 'Was I acting strangely and was I alone? Perhaps it was a multiple car crash I had caused and not reported. Not remembered either.' I shook my head and tugged my hair to the ever increasing questions I generated.

'I may have sliced through a worm when I was digging but for Christ's sake they nabbed me planting sweet fucking peas and charged me with murder,' I shouted for anyone to hear.

'Swearing shows you're under stress, assumes guilt,' shouted the duty officer. 'You'll be advised of developments as soon as we have them.'

'Ahha, as soon as we have them. Really? Huh... Don't I deserve to be stressed? I'll tell you why. Not only did I not murder anyone, the system is not right. I've seen enough police procedures on telly to know something's not kosher. I tell you that if there's no court appearance on Monday, I'll create merry hell. Mark my words.'

2

I WAS GLAD IT WAS MONDAY. EVERYONE WAS.

Staff had probably enjoyed their relaxing weekend. They'd be ready to jump into the new week and move my case on. That was my hope. I stretched out my arms, raised myself up on my toes and held a deep breath. A few moments later I relaxed, let my lungs empty and felt ready and optimistic to face the new day.

'Your breakfast,' announced the turnkey. She was a woman in her mid thirties in a smart white uniform shirt, highly polished black boots and dark navy trousers. The police did everything to de-sex a woman police officer. Only when she came into my cell did she show her femininity. She smiled as she handed the tray over. I interpreted her politeness as a precursor to an apology. I'd soon be out. She said nothing. She didn't have to. In that smile I detected a welcome friendly overture, as a male turnkey stood outside, just in case I flipped.

I gave the bowl of flakes and the buttered toast my full attention. I was preparing for the legal battle of my life. A full stomach was essential.

There was activity shortly after nine. I had expected it. A shuffling of feet, a few curses and shouts, the din ignited those prisoners still in their locked cells. The young men were preparing to face the Sheriff. Many had already done so in the not too distant past, I gathered from their occasional derisory outbursts. One by one the local offending community shuffled by, having changed back into the clothes they had been picked up in, at the weekend.

It seemed more staff was on duty to cope with the movement. Noisy chatter grew louder. I couldn't hear what they were saying. Then I heard and saw them come along the cell row. They were not all police officers. Some were Group Four prison escort staff. They had a different swagger about them.

My cell door was unlocked and a police officer gave me my clothes. I smiled. My shirt had been cleaned, and ironed. The gardening trousers had lost their knee dirt and looked very presentable. My shoes had been polished as well. I received them without laces.

'When you're dressed you'll get them back,' said one of the policemen acknowledging, by a smile, it was a rule. It was not likely I'd string myself up on his watch. I felt good, less of a criminal and looking respectable again. I'd soon be home and of course time to prepare to sue the police for wrongful detention. I could get a relaxing Caribbean holiday out of this, I thought. Well maybe not but at least a London show or two on a freebie visit.

As I bent down to lace and tie my shoes, I was aware of three Group Four staff eyeing me.

'Jack Watson?' I heard, reminding me of the morning class register all those years ago at school.

'Yes.'

'We're taking you to Glasgow Airport.'

'Wait…What the fuck are you saying?' I said stressing the F word in their faces.

'Just following orders, Jack. Don't make matters worse for yourself. The Crown Office is satisfied you can go,' the man said with a sneer developed from confronting such awkward customers.

'The bloody Crown Office says I can go? How kind of the buggers. Go where?' I shouted feeling my blood boil.

'An extradition warrant has been issued. They agreed to it,' said the Group Four man reading from his notes.

'Extradition agreed? God, where to? North Korea perhaps? Yea that's the place, I'm sure. Isn't it? Whatever his name is you know Kim Sun something found me on Facebook and thought he'd cover up his dirty work and accuse me. That's what it's all about. Pyongyang, here I come. Tell me, that's where the bodies lie, surely? That's the murder charge, yeah? I committed this murder in North Korea. Of course I did. How could I have forgotten?' My outburst had been the most vitriolic and ironic I'd ever spouted. I was not proud of what came out of my mouth. I realised I had ranted like a runaway train, now slowing down, braking to hear more.

'You are being flown to Florida.'

'Florida?' Not for the first time had I heard that locus. I felt a cold sweat break out yet images of blue seas spouting white waves burning under an oven hot sky filled my mind. It's a wind up I concluded. This is a prank that's gone too far. Bet they won't even get me to the van. I played alongside them. That could be the only explanation.

'I've never been in Florida... no, not Florida, I'm sure, I think, anyway. No, it was not in Florida.'

The prank faded from my thoughts as I saw the handcuffs appear once more. I could not resist them. There was no point. 'Some corpse you have out there,' I said in a quieter voice. They did not acknowledge the suggestion. I grew impatient. 'For God's sake, either call this whole con off or sort this out before I fly.'

'That might not be possible, sir,' the Group Four Security driver said, straightening his tie.

'Why ever not?' I pleaded.

'Your flight leaves in an hour and a half. We'd better be on our way.'

This was becoming serious. A spider's web was slowly trapping me. The more I struggled, the more I got entangled. I felt really frustrated, unable to escape.

I was taken to an isolated lounge still in handcuffs. Airports till now had always thrilled me. I loved their clicking destination boards. I was sure I would be on a plane full of holiday makers, heading for the Sunshine State. Then two dark suited men approached.

'Sir, we are flying to Florida, Tallahassee on the Gulf of Mexico. Nonstop flight, any questions?'

'You do know... I've never been to Florida? Anyway, I've not brought my passport.'

'Don't worry about the passport sir, you won't need one. About your case, we have almost no knowledge. Our duty is to bring you to the court in Tallahassee, no more than that. Co-operate with us and the handcuffs can come off and we enjoy the flight. By the way, my name's Chuck.'

'I'm Wayne,' perked up the smaller of the two men. 'We're both ex US Army SEALs.'

I acknowledged them proffering my clasped hands to shake theirs and smiling. 'Seems like I'm no further forward in this mess. I can assure you two, this sixty-five year old just ain't going to put up a fight. I'll keep my fight for the court.'

A key released my wrists and I gently rubbed them, letting the blood flow unrestricted. My protectors smiled at me. An easy flight waited, perhaps even the prospect of a good in-flight movie too.

A door flew open. Our heads turned. A middle-aged suited man approached, breathing hard.

'Excuse me. I'm a defence lawyer, Gordon Massey.' He showed his Law Society of Scotland identification. 'Can I have a word with Mr Watson, in private?'

'You got eight minutes, max.' Wayne pointed to his watch then tapped it twice with his index finger.

'God am I pleased to see you? Can you get me out of this?' I said with hope etched all over my face.

'Hang on. The Crown Office asked me to see you.'

'That's the bloody outfit extraditing me,' I smarted.

Mr Massey raised his right hand to stop me saying more. 'Yes, I know. Okay, have you had any mental health issues?'

'Not till this weekend. No, not really.'

'What do you mean, not really?' asked Gordon.

'I had to give up work because I got MCI. You know, mild cognitive impairment.'

'Dementia?'

'Sort of, dementia's wee brother. It might go that way later or just stay the same. Time will tell.'

'So how does it affect you?'

'Long term memory great; short term memory faulty.'

'What was your work?'

'I was the regional reporter to the children's hearings.'

'So you know about the law?'

'The law for children, yes. How is that going to help?'

'Frankly I need anything to try to prevent you flying off today. Anything else?'

'High blood pressure and pills to avert another seizure. Tennis elbow, weak knees… that's about it.'

Gordon's pen was as active as his brain. The lines filled his page very quickly. He looked at his watch. Four minutes remained. Chuck and Wayne sat nearby, nursing cardboard coffee cups.

'Must phone, hang on… Crown Office…' Gordon turned and walked a pace or two away. He was out of my earshot.

I was pleased he was getting back to them and wondered if he had sufficient health issues to prevent me flying. Not only that, perhaps showing I'd be a useless witness. God, no, I'm not the witness. I'm the bloody accused.

Gordon returned switching off his phone.

'I'm sorry Jack. They won't budge. They have had too many cases withheld from them and the Yanks are getting itchy with us. They don't see your memory loss as enough to keep you here. It's not Alzheimer's disease let alone normal dementia. There is a history of not letting many go to face justice in America and that's what has sealed it for you. So, do you know anything about this murder? How do you plead?'

'Gordon, I've been wracking my brains since Friday. I wasn't there and I've got no motive to kill anyone. I don't even know the deceased. Not guilty, I assure you.'

He nodded and seemed to be sucking an invisible lemon sherbet. 'Then I don't think you have to worry. It will be over some identity error. Your case will be hard for them to prove from what you say. DNA, new technologies, they've got it all over there. They should work in your favour.'

'Thanks. Best piece of news I've had so far. Why couldn't it be sorted out when I was arrested?'

'Murder with an extradition order, it's too sensitive a case Jack. If anyone gets it wrong they might lose their job. The local police are not familiar with the procedure; they need the advice of senior colleagues. The police pass it on to the Crown Office. They put it on to me to find any last chance. I'm afraid, that's it.'

'Have you seen the actual details of the charge?' I asked.

'No, only what you know. The Americans haven't shared that with me. They say they have evidence to charge you with murder. That's all we know. Sounds serious I agree, but it will fall on identity. Take my word for it. Come on Jack, chin up.'

Gordon rose and patted my shoulder. I smiled. He was the first to be on my side. I hoped he wasn't the last.

'Are you joining us on the flight?' I asked in vain hope.

'Not this flight. In two months' time I'll be having a family holiday in Florida. By that time, you'll be back home Jack.'

3

WE WERE LAST TO BOARD, INEVITABLE I
SUPPOSE.

It was of course the back row too, out of sight but
near the loo. Presumably the crew knew that two SEALs
were aboard with a murderer. I sat between them on the
port side of the plane. Above the headrest in front of me
I saw a burly man wedge a broad rimmed sunhat into
the overhead hold.

'Don't squash it darling,' I heard his wife plead. He
did not reply. Instead he held a stare which showed the
anger of a husband being reprimanded in public.

I looked out of the window towards the Glasgow
terminal. When would I see my city again? Would I
ever see Scotland again? Didn't Florida retain the death
penalty? For the next few hours I would be a prisoner
wedged between two giant law enforcers. I had better
get used to this comfortable imprisonment. I hoped I'd
not get bored or frustrated at being book-ended by my
minders. There was nothing I could do to resolve my
case in this setting. I relaxed.

A young blond head appeared popping up above the
headrest like a toaster ejecting the bread. The freckled

face smiled at us. I think we all smiled back.

'Who are you?' the cocky lad asked. Before the other two could think of a suitable reply, I chipped in.

'We are three astronauts.' I sensed my seat mates turn towards me without giving away their incredulity with my response.

'Have you been on the moon?' the boy asked.

'I've been round the moon. I've gone round the world too, some forty times. We do experiments in the weightlessness of space.'

The boy's eyes lit up. He was onto a winner. He disappeared.

'One lie leads to another,' Wayne whispered.

'It's not me lying. Whoever framed me is the lying crook. I'm only widening the horizon of a youngster. What a story he will have to tell at school, meeting not one but three astronauts. It might start an essay and could even make him an author one day, like me.'

'So you're a writer?'

'Yup, published quite a few books.'

'What type?' asked Chuck somewhat impressed.

'Mainly novels; some children's books too.'

'Novels, how many?

'Nine now.'

'What's your latest?' enquired Wayne.

'The Crazy Psychologist.'

'Any crime novels?' asked Chuck.

'Oh yes. Real crime. Not like this stitched up affair.'

The young head appeared again with a piece of paper torn from his mother's diary.

'Can I have your autographs please?' he asked politely handing the paper and a pen over the headrest.

I smiled at the lad. He was on my surreal wavelength. I drew a large circle of a full moon and printed my name around the circumference, then my scrawling signature as a line beneath. I refrained from adding 'murderer' though it did cross my mind. Wayne received the paper. He drew a rocket with a thrust launching pose and then an indecipherable signature. Chuck took the paper and signed his name. He was not the creative sort. He seemed a practical hands-on man and I felt I'd have his hands grasping my collar when the flight was over.

The boy disappeared like a descending periscope. Then a moment later his mother stood up and came round to acknowledge our co-operation with her son's request.

'A pleasure madam,' I said thinking some common courtesy was needed in my life. I hoped it might rub off on my captors.

'So you are not all Americans?' she asked.

'No, I'm a Glaswegian. Chuck is from Nebraska and Wayne from Klamath Falls, Oregon. That so boys?'

They nodded with lowered brows. They clearly could not have imagined coming from either of these States I mentioned. Then their eyes lit up. The aisle trolley was approaching with lunch.

It was half an hour before we landed that I first noticed it. It started with a faint smell, something not very pleasant and increasing in magnitude. The air was stale as though filled by an approaching invisible putrid cloud, coming from an engine, I assumed. The poor quality of air was concentrated. Oxygen masks descended onto our laps and that increased the blood pressure of passengers. I heard some groans. It eased our breathing but something unexplained was affecting the air quality and the crew had no answers. Perhaps they knew too much and did not want to cause anxiety by sharing their knowledge. Sickness bags were distributed and began to fill. I looked at my watch. We were due to land in twelve minutes.

Chuck was pale. He was not coping and soon had his sick bag in use. I too felt queasy. Was it the smell or my anxiety at approaching America? The foul air seemed an unlucky omen to what would follow for me on landing. Yet it could also be my saviour if it led to an unconscious state. Even death for me was a viable option at that moment.

When we touched down many passengers applauded the safe landing. All exits were quickly opened to expel the toxic air. The engines shut down soon afterwards. The fresh air entered the craft at a good rate. An ambulance had been summoned for three elderly travellers who had floated in and out of consciousness. Perhaps there was still time to feign that perhaps. Yes, I could maybe gain some precious thinking time. I shook my head. Not worth the bother really. The sooner I confronted the American legal system the better.

'Well, I hope your space flights go better than this experience. Safe landings to you all. I'll be following the space programme much more closely having met three astronauts. Gentlemen, it has been a pleasure speaking to and meeting you.'

'The pleasure has been all ours madam and thanks for the good wishes. We astronauts like to have good folks like you behind us,' I said in a calm and polite manner. I felt an elbow in my side. Chuck was still feeling miserable and he really did hate small talk.

As the young boy passed by smiling, I gave him a seated salute. The boy stopped and saluted us back, then leaned over to shake the hands of the three celebrity spacemen. All three of us obliged, entering into the spirit of the scene, to conclude our one act play.

The plane was empty now. Wayne checked his mobile then spoke to a driver requesting him to approach the back of the plane. As we stood up, out came the handcuffs.

'Are these really necessary? I'm hardly going to run away in a strange land at my age.'

'Mandatory, Jack. No more than that, mandatory.' Chuck felt awkward in locking the cuffs. He probably had a father of my age.

I walked into an oven of warm air and the smells of a new environment. The sea air mingled with mild rotting vegetation. It assaulted my nasal senses. That was my first impression of Tallahassee, a place where sun block and sun glasses would be ubiquitous. We were all glad to be off the plane able to revert to normality. No more acting required. My protectors were pleased because their duties were almost over; as for me, I was anxious to get greater clarity about my situation.

The car that attended took us only a few miles beyond the airport where a state trooper's car awaited. Cool air-conditioning sharpened my thinking. I was tempted to thank Chuck and Wayne for their good company. I couldn't. They left in an unsatisfactorily quick manner. They were out of sight as I entered the car. My new minder was Bill Tucson, uniformed and armed with a pistol and a pencil thin moustache. Both looked menacing. He sat with me in the back of the car as we approached the centre of Tallahassee.

'Where am I heading now, may I ask?'

'The holding bay. You will have a lawyer attached to your case, for your Court appearance tomorrow.'

'And can you enlighten me about how I am connected to this murder?' I asked with politeness.

'Didn't ya hear me? I said you will have a lawyer, tomorrow,' he growled.

I adjusted my watch. There seemed no point in pressing or engaging this officer. He wouldn't know why I was with him. His orders would have been brief and to the point. No knowledge was good knowledge it seemed for him. Not for me. I sat back in the car watching the pace of the city, a city with a heartbeat going too fast for my comfort or liking.

The holding bay was much more relaxed. It did have high security yet I was on remand and allowed to enter a hall where table tennis and a basket ball court were situated. Presumably whether guilty or innocent, if high powered exercise could be provided, the testosterone levels would diminish and prisoners would be manageable. I met one British man whose name was printed on his orange jump suit. He was a well spoken individual, a Londoner I thought, keen to talk to me.

'They boarded my boat. Found drugs heading for Europe. I could be looking at a long stretch here. Not sure if I can face it. What charge are you on?'

'Well Brian, it's not one I'm proud of either. They think they've got me for murder.'

'Christ, you had better get a good lawyer or the electric chair might be coming your way. This is Florida,' he said. Then a smirk came over his lips. 'Mind you, that puts my case in a better light. Even if I get thirty years, I'll come out alive,' he said as if he had found a palatable sentence after all. They put us in the same cell that night. I didn't learn much more about him. I was dead beat tired. I slept like a helpless child.

Dave Felder was my appointed lawyer. A Public Defender as he was called as I had no lawyer to defend me. He was a man with determination in his eyes and when we met, he looked at his papers. I tried to engage him to break the ice. He didn't respond. He seemed to be engrossed in my case notes.

Tall and lean, a degree effeminate I thought, yet he had the authority that was necessary for me. He gave me a degree of confidence. I was aware he was a man with his client's case to the fore of his mind. Perhaps arrogant to a degree but at least he was my only stateside advocate. I had better make good use of him. He explained my first appearance would be short. The court had to establish the fact that the accused had been detained. All I had to do was acknowledge who I was. Of course, of that I was quite certain. The judge would also question why

I had been detained. The M word would seal further incarceration, pending progress.

'Tell me, who is it I allegedly murdered?' I asked with bewilderment, feeling at last I could clarify why a sweet pea planter found himself behind bars in Florida within hours of detention.

'It was a very brutal murder, Jack, caused a lot of local sympathy.' He handed me the photograph of the murder scene.

'God, what a killing. What a messy scene. That's horrible. The murderer must have been out of his mind. Oh come on, that's just not me. I could never have caused that. There's no way I did that.'

'The victim was a naturalised American. Mr Gary McFaul. You heard of him?'

I opened my mouth, no words came out. Daniel McGraw no, it wasn't. They got the name wrong. Not Daniel 'Danny' McGraw at all but Daniel Gary McFaul... Gary... McFaul. I experienced two powerful emotions. They could be seen in both my eyes and in my colour. I had gone pale. My heart rate increased and a cold shiver ran down my back. I was stiff, my body locked. I was in shock.

I turned to Dave slowly. I looked him in the eye. 'So, wrong name. Not Daniel McGraw after all. Oh God. I don't believe this. You mean Daniel Gary McFaul don't you... yes... he was known simply as Gary McFaul?'

Dave nodded 'Gary McFaul, yes. You knew him?'

Beads of sweat on my forehead gathered in a congregation of confusion. 'I've known him all my life. But I did not murder him. And I'm not sure if that pleases me or not,' I found myself saying in no more than a whisper.

Dave took some notes, with a gold-topped pen. He scribbled away some more before he continued to enlighten me.

'Gary met a gruesome death, as you can see. One of the worst I've ever seen.'

'A gruesome end? You said it. Come on, you think I did it?'

Dave pouted his lips. 'The court will decide, Jack. How much you were involved is very much at the heart of this case.'

I felt a cold shiver in the sub tropical heat. 'You are kidding me,' I said wondering if everyone was conspiring to catch me out, determined that I should be fed to the lions.

'Okay, listen, Jack. The police have a body, a badly injured body. That means the next of kin has to be informed. They go to his house and break the sad news to his wife, Sal. She goes crazy, naturally. You can imagine that. After a few minutes the police ask who could have killed her husband. Who bore a grudge? Who could have murdered Gary McFaul, her husband?'

'Okay I'm following.' I felt sorry for Sal, just for a moment.

'And then she gave your name.'

'What? My name?'

'Yes, she says you have been hounding Gary for years. Is that the case?'

I had to think clearly. God, I needed to think hard through the past few months, indeed the past few years and see how it all fitted together. It would not be easy. Could some things make sense at last? I recognised I was now in trouble and needed Dave, the only one on my side in the American court system. I needed confidence to tell him more.

'You are wrong that I have hounded him for years, wrong on two counts in fact. Finding justice is not hounding. And it was not over some years, as she says. It was three years apart.' My mind had not been clearer for several hours.

'Jack, we need to talk.'

Dave nodded silently twiddling his pen between his fingers.

4

THE COURT IN DOWNTOWN TALLAHASSEE was a colonial styled red brick building. Its internal corridors were the ones I encountered. I was led into the court and sat at a table with Dave. He filled a tumbler of water and gave it to me. I did not drink any. The air conditioning made me shiver. The drooping American flag by the side of the bench brightened up the court, but its solemn stance reminded me of the seriousness of the charge I would face. Was this the place I was going to be tried and found guilty? Or would I leave this court one day a free man? Without knowing what the prosecuting attorney's box of evidence looked like, my future seemed to be at the mercurial spin of a dime.

The Arraignment Proceedings were remarkably brief. My name, my temporary address and date of birth were recorded. I informed the Judge that I was pleading not guilty and I was remanded, as I had expected. The procedure was over before I had taken in the quiet atmosphere and dignity of the actors on their stage.

I returned from court to holding-status, not where I had been prior. I was sent to the Tallahassee Correctional

Institution. This was a real prison with real convicts. Due to my age, I was placed with the elderly long termers along with most of the untried prisoners of my age. I don't know if they were high on dope or low on energy through daily drudgery because there was hardly a spark amongst my new cell mates.

The regime assumed anyone who was sent to them needed correction and that went for the untried prisoners too. Isolation had a double effect on me. Long periods locked up in a two man cell were claustrophobic yet the time gave me an opportunity to understand the road which I had travelled through my life and which had brought me to this precipice. The fears of my childhood, the direction life had taken me away from loved ones, the determination to overcome feelings of self doubt and the failure to cleanse my mind of the past. Yet it was not a life of abject failure. My wife Joan had been my rock, my lover and confidant. She had given me strength when I needed it. My work pleased many and it gave me satisfaction. Was it, however, what I was originally cut out to be?

I had to get the story right, verifiable and unambiguous to Dave's ear and he promised an urgent interview. It came two days later.

We sat in a comfortable if small room set aside for lawyers to consult clients. Dave had booked the room for two hours. It was longer than usual and the staff had commented negatively on that fact. Dave arrived in a short sleeved lime shirt, tieless and bronzed. I imagined his drop seat Porsche coupé was parked in the lot outside.

His success oozed from his fashion specs to the gold leaf bracelet on his right wrist and his expensive Breitling wristwatch. This man had an expensive taste. He got straight down to the business of my case. I liked that.

'So how did you know the late Gary McFaul?'

I took a deep soulful breath.

'We attended the same school in Glasgow, Albany Academy on the north west side of town.'

'State school?'

I laughed for the first time in American custody. 'Culture clash here. It's a public fee-paying school. Not open to the public. Except my Dad was classified in one of the less remunerative professions, he was a pastor, so I was heading for a minimal fee. I won a scholarship however so Dad didn't have to pay after all.'

'Bright kid then?'

'Prize winner every year, I was. Some years it was just general knowledge and maths, in other years languages and science too. However the second year was my last winning season. I took four prizes that year including music. Three more years then I would be off to university and a profession to follow. Maybe be a pastor like my dad or a dentist or doctor like my uncles. The world was my oyster and I knew I was fortunate. My smile faded. 'No, it just wasn't like that. No way. A massive fall from grace was underway. I had won my last prize.'

Dave looked puzzled. 'Okay, I get that, so what happened?'

'I warn you, I must give you the complete story. I can't miss any out. It's all about this case. It might take some time. Are you happy with that?'

Dave returned his pen to his shirt pocket. From his briefcase he took out a recording device. It was a neat oblong, small, black device. He placed it between us. He switched it on.

'One hour each side. We'll have a break after the first.' He leant back in his chair. He coupled his hands behind his head.

My chair grunted as I brought it nearer to the recorder. I didn't want it to miss any sentence I was about to share.

'Okay, go for it Jack. I'm listening and I'll get a transcript when it's over.'

I took a big sigh and my fingers combed through my hair. I knew I had to get every word right.

'Gary lived in the road parallel to mine, about a three minute walk between our houses. He was at least two and a half years older.' I smiled. 'He was always two and a half years older, the only son of a surgeon. I suspected he'd follow his father's profession. Anyway, he started to waylay me. He pinned me against a tree once and leant on me. I froze. He had complete control over me. I didn't know how to react. Fortunately, I saw my mother coming back from the town on that occasion and that got him off me pretty damn quick. I felt powerless since this lad was a good bit taller as well as older.'

'Did you tell anyone what happened?' asked Dave leaning back after speaking over his recorder.

'Not at that time. What was there to report? I'm talking about the summer of 1964… maybe 1965.'

'Hang on.' Dave raised his hand to attract the attention of the guard who regularly looked through the wire-meshed window panes of the interview rooms. He waved him in.

'Two coffees please. What do you take Jack?'

'No milk, one sugar, thanks.'

'Sir, inmates don't get coffee. I'll bring you one,' the guard looked at me and grinned.

'Officer, just a minute.' Dave pointed to the chair I was sitting on. 'What if you were sat there with a thought of one door leading to the outside world and the other to the electric chair? If I was your lawyer and got you a coffee would you appreciate that?'

The penny dropped. His weight moved from one foot to the other. 'Two coffees then, against the rules,' he said reinforcing his opposition to the request as he left abruptly.

Dave turned to me and winked. This lawyer had influence. I liked the way he used it.

'Okay, Gary, so you are telling me he's grooming you.'

'Yes. He followed me home every day. There was safety in numbers usually. On most occasions he waited under the station bridge till I was alone. He was frightening me and I had no way of getting rid of him. He followed like a cunning fox and when he got me he clung on like a sea limpet. Then one day his mother telephoned my mother and I was invited to go over to Gary's house to see his train set.' Dave saw me tremble as I revealed this information.

'I wouldn't go. I had an argument with my mother who could not understand why I would not go and see his electric train set. My own train was clockwork, clumsy and always taking the corners at too much speed. I remembered my cumbersome metal clockwork train foretelling future train crashes as it launched itself with regularity off the rails and into the skirting board.'

This image remained in my mind as I continued to tell Dave about my association with the deceased.

'In those days, being a thirteen year old, arguing with parents was not done. We were to be seen and not heard. My mother must have seen my unease. But what could she do? She could not understand what I was going through. I remained obedient to her and so made the biggest mistake of my life, I went to his house.'

The door opened and not only did the tray have two coffees, it held chocolate chip cookies too on a plate.

'Eat up,' smiled Dave knowing his influence with the staff was working very well indeed, for he was a competent lawyer, dour at times but clever. That's what I needed in a lawyer.

My hand trembled as I held the hot drink. I steadied it by resting it on my lower lip with two hands before taking two sips of the coffee. It invigorated me. It sharpened my focus.

'So, I got to his house and Gary told his mother we would play with the trains. We went up to this room. It was situated on the left hand side of the staircase. It would be a spare bedroom for anyone else but for Gary, it was his train room. This only child rattled in such a large stone mansion and he had been given the room to erect a large table on which a community lived. The streets were in clear detail, a church, a school and of course a railway station. One train sat at the station. Gary started the electric train and as it progressed around the miniature town, he set off another train heading in the opposite direction, on a parallel track. I was transfixed with the reality of the setting, mesmerised by the progress of two trains on two different tracks. It captivated me. The trains made a realistic noise and that sound filled the room. It was what he had planned. I can still hear it, hear it so vividly. And the smell of electricity and oil from the tracks remains stored in my head, trapped in my memory with no escape. Fed on anger, it still thrives to this day, an obnoxious smell which makes me want to vomit.

Then I heard the door handle. I turned round and a chair was being lodged against the internal door. I felt cold fear. A fear of such magnitude I had not experienced before. A fear that brought despair, a portent of something bad, something nasty was about to happen, I knew not what. I felt a brittle chilling of my body. The grooming, though I did not know the word at the time, was about to enter a new phase.'

I removed my glasses and held my forehead. Tears welled up in my eyes. Dave said nothing, letting the moment pass. It took a moment in time.

'That's when it happened. Stripped by him, he stripped himself far quicker. He was physically mature. I wasn't. I lacked pubic hair. I had not seen a naked adult person before, of either sex. This was the early 60s. He handled me then pulled and rubbed me to a painful groan. The conclusion was excruciating pain and non-productive. I had of course no idea what he was expecting for I was still months away from my first nocturnal emission. He was now erect and masturbating against me. I did not understand that this was possible and stepped back as soon as his volatile sperm hit me just below my chest. I did not know this was masturbation. I only knew I did not like what he was doing. The power over me he had. I was in shock and I knew it was not right.'

I took another sip of coffee and ate a biscuit without moving my eyes from the table.

'Take your time, Jack.'

I offered a faint smile. Dave noticed my falling tears. He gave me a tissue.

I resumed emptying my memory. 'Then I heard his mother at the door. She tried the handle and immediately the resistance made her curious. The door rattled. When she managed to dislodge the chair, the door opened. Gary was standing in front of me.

'Gary, for goodness sake, what are you doing?' she shouted, with her hands over her mouth when she saw her son naked and erect. 'And is Jack like that too?' She peered round her son to see the immature naked me, appearing from underneath the train table.

'I warn you right now. Your father will deal with you when he comes home tonight, Gary. Now get dressed immediately.' Hearing me sobbing she offered me a sympathetic smile.

'Come down for some juice, when you are dressed,' she said realising this was her reason to come to the room in the first place.

'I lost no time. I grabbed my underwear and dressed faster than I thought possible. That is what happened. So we went down and outside. It was summer. His dog Rex was a golden retriever, a breed which oozes love and I received unconditional love from that dog at that moment as I stroked him. I needed just that. One hand patted him and I ran my hand over his ears to his delight. I half drank the juice with Gary sat on the same wooden bench smiling at me. I did not stay to eat any biscuit despite seeing they were irresistibly chocolate-coated. I got up and ran out of that garden and back home without saying any word.'

The silence between us was shaken by a scream from a landing above.We instinctively both looked up at the ceiling. Dave looked at his recorder. He placed it even nearer me.

'So Jack, how often did it happen after that first time?'

My brows gathered. I was angry.

'That's the point, God dam it. My life, my whole raison d'être was now devoted to avoiding this man who lived so near to me and attended the same school. You have no idea how my life changed from that moment. Yes, it was only one abusive occasion but a devastating moment as you will discover.'

'Tell me Jack. This is important. You are shedding new light on this case.'

I nodded in agreement as I stared into his face.

'Naturally I would see him every day at school. Getting to school was not so hard. Trains were packed with pupils from different schools and men and women heading to town to fill offices. At the end of the day at 4pm it was different. I had to avoid him at all costs so I loitered in large shops in town before getting a later train home. Sometimes I took the bus home not getting off at the presumed place. On other times I took the train to the stop after or the stop before my usual station. It meant a longer walk home most days but this way I would avoid seeing him wait for me under the station bridge. Planning how to get safely home became a strategic operation each and every day for me, and in all weathers. The planning was done as I sat in maths, physics, French... every day. That was the first effect of that black summer afternoon.' I took a further drink and wiped my mouth with the back of my hand.

'Did your parents not suspect something was wrong?'

'No, they never asked and I never told because I did not know the words to describe what happened nor understand; why it was making my life feel so different, so badly different. Then the first report card appeared after the event. My father could not understand it. Neither could my teachers. I was no longer shining academically in any subject or in any class. Some teachers thought I was losing concentration, for whatever reason, they did not know. A very perceptive assessment they made. If only they had probed deeper. Yet even if they had and found out what had happened, I doubt whether they would have acted in those days.'

'You sure were affected,' said Dave.

'Yes, I certainly was. It was a fall from academic grace of seismic proportions and it continued. You might have thought when Gary left school and went off to university to study history in the north of England, my arch enemy would disappear from my life. If only. At Easter, summer holidays and Christmas he would be at home a few hundred yards away. Thoughts of him appalled me and I could not get his abuse of me out of my system no matter how much I tried. It was at that time I took up the accordion. I knew Gary was not musical at all. I loved the sound it made and I played it at every opportunity. It rested against my chest and breathed its bellows in time with mine. It was a comforter and I needed its voice to speak for me, for I was seized by verbal silence at times.'

'Okay, I get the picture. I think you need a break Jack.'

'Please no, there's a lot more you will find hard to believe. Honestly, there is.'

'Okay, if you are up to it, sure.'

'You know, to have someone listen to me is so cathartic.' I realised this to be a golden opportunity to off load my permanent anxiety and I knew how rarely such opportunities would come my way. I took a mouthful of coffee, and another cookie. Then I was ready to continue.

'When it came to the important exams, I failed all but one subject, English. I was able to pass that one without too much work. It left me behind as I had to sit the exams again and my class friends progressed to do their higher level qualifications while I struggled to make sense of basic education. I left the following year with the minimum grades to do a three year social work certificate course in Edinburgh. It would be a job in which I could work with children who might have suffered like me. Gary would hopefully not know I had left Glasgow.

However there were holiday times when confrontation might occur. My opportunity to seek further safety from him over the summer months appeared on the college notice board. For two consecutive summers, as a student, I went to Camp America. I was sent to Camp Onota in the Berkshire Hills of Massachusetts. That was where I could for the first time feel really relaxed. I made many friends and one in particular became a clinical psychologist who was to feature in my life many, many years later. When the summers ended, I returned to my parental home. After three years I qualified. Now I had to work somewhere. The Western Isles came to mind but Scotland was small and I feared our lives might cross again. There was only one solution which could answer my anxieties and so I brazenly entered their head office. I walked into the Church of Scotland headquarters in Edinburgh and asked to serve as a social worker abroad, in their overseas division.'

I smiled at that point as this had been my largest victory over Gary. Not only was the close proximity of our homes gone, we'd be continents apart.

'As I was not a declared adherent of the Church however, the basic requirement of a missionary candidate, I was sent to St Colms' Missionary College in Edinburgh and took the required course to be admitted into that bastion of the Church. My motivation, as you can tell, was not spiritual or evangelical in any way, more one based on survival through distance, an expression of flight. The Mission Field welcomed me, an unlikely, grateful, yet dishonest adherent.'

'That was a big decision and I can see why,' Dave said placing his clasped hands behind his head and leaning back, I nodded for almost twenty seconds as I recalled that momentous decision. I must have seemed I was completely switched off.

'It was to Ghana, they sent me. And there I met my wife who was a chemistry teacher in the country. And there I played rugby first for Accra and then for Ghana against Nigeria and Sierra Leone. Standing on the touchline one Saturday was Professor Hunter from London University's School of Oriental and African Studies. At the end of the game, he approached to congratulate me on our team's victory over Nigeria. Then he asked about my work. I told him that I was now employing a Ghanaian to take over my work in the Industrial Mission in Tema and we would soon face an uncertain future. Professor Hunter was impressed with what I was doing and offered me a place, there and then, at London University to do a post graduate course in African studies. I told him, I could not do a post graduate degree course without having done a graduate course. I just had a certificate in social work. He assured me I could cope with the work. And that meant a post-graduate year in London ending with graduation in the Royal Albert Hall. A degree at last some ten years after I should have obtained one. And I'll just say one thing more at this stage. After graduation, I thought the only job I could do was to ensure other abused children were properly treated. I could understand their victimisation, scape-goating, blame and bullying. So I became a children's reporter.'

'A children's reporter? What did that involve?' he asked squinting at me to understand a post not known to him.

'Offending children and the victims of physical, emotional or sexual abuse would be referred to me by the police, school or parent. I would request reports of the child from his or her school and from a social worker, then I had to make a decision whether to take action by arranging a hearing which could lead to supervision at home, in the community or in secure accommodation. Other cases included freeing young children for adoption or fostering. It's the legal process for children's cases in Scotland. And I did that till I retired, in 2013.'

'Thirty six years or so?' asked Dave.

'Yes, I retired a bit early. Not something I wanted. I was having memory problems. I assumed I was under stress and the doctor would give me time off to unwind and resume work. But I was sent for tests. I met my first psychoanalyst then. He informed me I had mild cognitive impairment. He also asked why I became a children's reporter and at that point I broke down. It took little time for him to realise my response opened a deep wound. He asked me to report my abuser to the police.'

'I understand just how devastating that afternoon must have been, no longer safeguarding unfortunate children.'

'Yes, and don't you realise the abuse stays with the victim for life and there are so many around, still suffering. The abuser on the other hand sees the dastardly offence as just one satisfying action, a gesture of unwelcomed love or just a mistake on their victim's part, now over and done with.'

I dried up for the time being and Dave turned off his recorder. 'Can we meet tomorrow?' he said returning his pen to his shirt pocket.

'My place or yours?' I grinned.

Dave laughed quietly. Then he leaned over and whispered.

'Jack, if this case wasn't so serious, you'd be a good stand up comic.'

I smiled. 'I hope I live to see the funny side of it too but that won't be tomorrow.'

'No, you are right there. It's still a very murky case,' he admitted regretting his last comment.

Dave gathered his case and possessions together.

'You have given me some homework. I'd better get down to it tonight.'

5

I FELT SURPRISINGLY GOOD, ALMOST LIKE
A man on the brink of freedom. Dave had given me
confidence. Yet there was still much to tell him. He had
to know the timeline of my life.

He seemed to be taking in what I had told him.
What he would make of this information was beyond
me but surely it was ammunition against my accusers.
Where it would lead was beyond my understanding. It
wasn't just Dave I had to totally convince. It was the
attorney-at-law who had brought the case against me.
She, I learned, was Ms Diane Inkster. That sounded a
Scandinavian name and if she went by form, that could
make her not only a tall blond perhaps, but a sensitive
individual too. That would be my hope. A vision of
Abba came to mind. Dave, take a chance on me, I found
myself humming.

I felt a little awkward meeting Dave the following day.
I had not had a shower and the heat of the morning
made me as clammy as a damp facecloth. I was informed
showers were for court days or every second day. I must
have arrived too late on a shower day.

'Hi Jack. My wife, Nancy, made some brownies for us. I'd better give some to the guys out there. Besides cookies without coffee are like salami without a knife.'

I settled down to our session with Dave opening his file which was now beginning to bulge.

'All my case papers?' I asked in bewilderment.

'Sure is. With my additional case law notes too. Enough to make a novel out of this,' suggested Dave.

'A novel. Why not a film? Which part would you take?'

'I like that dog Rex,' Dave growled.

'So did I, boy, so did I.'

Two coffees arrived without prompting and a delighted guard retired with a half dozen chocolate brownies.

'Well, as I said, I was a children's reporter. One day late in my career, I left the gas station and forgot to pay. I also got a bit lost around town and I put it all down to stress. I was president of the Robert Burns Club and I had also been made the chair of the Child Protection committee for the region. I'd taken on board a little too much work. I had self diagnosed stress. So I made an appointment with my GP, hoping I'd be given four months – even six months off work to get myself together again. I'd catch up on some reading, especially on wet days, walk the dog more, tidy the garden and by then I'd be fit to get back to work. Others I had known had taken that route. I'd be the same.

However the doctor sent me for tests. I was sent to a psychoanalyst guy who probed a fair bit. He was impressed with me being the region's authority reporter and asked me why I decided to do that job. That's when, after a hesitation, the tears began to fall. He had no idea he had hit a raw nerve. All the abuse came out. He told me to contact the police. At that time I had no idea where Gary was but his cousin, an adopted cousin in fact, was a very keen darts player. The BBC had asked him to commentate on some international matches between Scotland and Norway. Good winter sporting entertainment. Then I realised if I contacted him, I could find out where Gary was. I found his cousin through BBC Scotland's sports desk. Of course he wondered why I wanted to contact him. Fortunately he answered his own question by asking if it was a school reunion I had in mind. Oh yes, that's what it's all about, I lied. Then when he told me Gary was a teacher of history in a boys' boarding school in Haverhill, Massachusetts, in New England, my mind went into overdrive. What better way to avail yourself of young boys than teach them and in a school with boarding facilities. I was able to furnish the local police with the details.'

'Good detective work there,' said Dave nodding his head. 'You could have been a policeman.'

'Thanks. But I doubt it.'

We earned a brief laid back sigh. 'Okay, let's get on with it. That is, if you are ready, Jack?'

'Sure. So I gave a full report to the local police. They told me the case would go to the chief in Boston. I heard nothing. Not that nothing happened. It's now obvious that Gary got wind of this. I have no idea how long he stayed in Haverhill. And I never heard anything more about it from the police.'

'So that's the 2013 investigation, leading nowhere. I'd love to search that one out sometime.'

'Yes, it would be good to know what happened. However it was the year 2013. Abuse was on a par with date rape. Specialist abuse officers were not employed in every police force. And of course when upstanding citizens were questioned with no corroborating evidence, the blind eye was turned. That's how it used to be. That's what makes victims like me contemplate suicide.'

'Jack, did you ever consider that?'

I hesitated. 'Suicide? Many do but not me. No, for two reasons. At the start, I was so preoccupied with avoidance I needed my wits about me. It kept me focussed and busy, so it never entered my mind. Not suicide anyway. Murder did come up as an option. The consequences, of course, were too dire. I could never murder anyone, except in my dreams. Gary dominated my subconscious state and I did murder him there. Now don't be making too much of that statement.'

Dave laughed. 'No evidence of death by dreaming.'

I smiled at Dave but I recalled the anguish of my dreams. I'd killed my adversary many times over.

'Seems murder is like a natural wish at times. Carrying it out is a different kettle of fish, ' I said wondering if what I had said, made sense.

Dave moved the meeting on. 'The other reason, Jack?'

I lifted the mug and sipped a little of the hot liquid. 'By then I had married the perfect woman. She was a listener, a comfort, a great friend and lover. I really miss her now.'

'Divorced?'

'No cancer, five years ago.'

'I'm sorry Jack.' he said patting my hand on the table.

'That's okay. I'm just glad she's not here with me, going through this hell.' I had to wipe a wandering tear from my eye. I did so with the sleeve of the blue boiler suit that remand prisoners wore in this correctional institution.

'I thought that was that. Police interviewed him at least. A warning, a cautionary piece of advice and a record kept just in case more evidence might emerge. A few weeks later however, I received a letter. It was from Gary's Massachusetts lawyer, a denial of course. His lawyer wrote that his client was a friend of mine and our relationship was based on friendship. I saw red. Living only 300 meters away, what sort of friendship existed when he never once visited my friendly family home? And how often did I visit his dwelling? Yes, once, that dreadful once. I tore the letter up. That's how I saw it settled and I felt yes, that's as much as I could and would do. Yet, still it niggled. Had he any idea of how it had changed my life? I doubted it. What about the school years of failure and the cat and mouse strategies, the summers I spent in Massachusetts at Camp America to distance myself from him and then my work in Ghana to get even further away? Then I became a children's reporter to help sad, difficult and abused children. Can you believe this? All these things happened as a result of one horrific afternoon. Amazing isn't it?

Repercussions in abuse stretch like the travelling flames of a bush fire. There was no further contact till 2015; no lengthy campaign against Gary. And it was not me who initiated the enquiries this time either. It was a different psychoanalyst.'

'So why a new investigation?' Dave asked adjusting his seated position to check the battery level of his recorder.

'I wrote a book. Hold on, the answer is coming I assure you. It's a complex maze this life I've led. It forced me down many different avenues. The novel is called The Crazy Psychologist and it is set on the Orkney island of Rousay in the far north of Scotland. My daughter is a senior specialist clinical psychologist. She made me think about the novel. I knew a few clinical psychologist friends too. Anyway I was asked to go to launch the book on Orkney's Rousay island. Then I thought I could invite my friend from Camp Onota days and his wife to join me. Both Lenny and Anna have doctorates in clinical psychology. I'd been in touch over the last three years via e-mail. Before they flew over however, I got an e-copy of the Albany School magazine. I get this these days as I returned to the school in 2006 to give a talk about my time in the North West Frontier Province of the Islamic Republic of Pakistan.'

'Good heavens. What were you doing there?'

'I was the camp manger, caring for twenty-four thousand victims of the 2005 earthquake. I've given quite a few schools an illustrated talk about this work over the past few years. I tell of how children lost everything; their parents, their homes.'

'I see. So, not really connected with the abuse or the school?'

'No, well yes and no. You see, that was my entry once more into the school of my youth.'

'Okay, I follow.'

'The school magazine is a good way to see the school develop, read about the activities of former pupils and it covers obituaries of former teaching staff and sometimes class mates. The magazine I got that day sent a shiver down my back. There was a coloured picture of the former school captain in 1967, he was visiting the school. He stood holding the shooting trophy he won that year. In the narrative beneath the picture it informed readers that Gary McFaul had visited and had now retired to Florida, in the southern United States, with his wife Sal.'

'I see, that's how the trail led down here.' Dave fitted the penultimate chess move into place. He leant back and smiled at me.

'Now you can imagine us, heading for Orkney, the long drive, the three of us telling stories, laughing at jokes and enjoying the different cultural exchanges. Lenny spoke of his unhappy childhood when maternal love was not in good supply. It affected his school marks. I then told him the similarities in my life as I have told you. That was when Anna told me sexual abuse was now being taken very seriously in the States as elsewhere. If my abuser had been a teacher then he would have placed many children at risk and he obviously wouldn't get work if they knew about him. He may have retired but he could be supplementing his income with private tutoring. Teaching, a very noble profession, can hide a den of seething vipers. In his wake, many children may still be suffering. So the process began anew, with a new residential location confirmed somewhere in Florida. On Anna's advice, I contacted the police again. The stakes were much higher and somehow Gary lost his life. He died shortly after the police took my second statement. That could mean someone was out to get him, and that someone wasn't me. My only regret was that he had died without knowing how cruelly he had acted and how his actions and grooming had changed my life forever. He being dead has not made the experience go away. I hope you see it was not a long drawn out campaign of oppression and accusation, as Sal makes out. It was two professionals, three years apart, who urged me to initiate proceedings and insisted that I should give a statement to the police, against Gary McFaul. I must make it perfectly clear I, personally, did not instigate the proceedings in either 2013 or 2015.'

'Sal's account sure has set this false trail ablaze. Your story can be checked through signed police statements of course. Seems like your memory is better than I expected, Jack.'

I smiled. 'Yes, but that's the long term memory. Ask me what I've done since arriving in America and I bet it's very sketchy.'

Dave looked at me assessing me and it felt awkward.

'There's something that doesn't add up,' he eventually said tapping his pen against his head. 'I must start with the police in Boston, Massachusetts.'

'Really, you don't believe me?' I asked.

'It may take a couple of days. Let's see if I can make your fortunes turn around, that's what I'm saying for the present, Jack.'

'Well, I am not going anywhere. You know where I am.'

I laughed. Dave didn't. He called the guard and I was led back to my cell. I felt drained and purged. But I also felt I had made a considerable impact on Dave and he seemed to be on the road to present my case history to the prosecuting attorney.

Prior to lunch the next day, an incident erupted. I was not initially sure if the heat of the day, hunger or drugs was responsible for it. Some fight broke out as suddenly as if a swarm of bees appeared. The ringleader was a large six foot seven black man and he had found an iron rod. He was going berserk, encouraged by his followers. He ran along the wing smashing the metal pole against cell doors. Then the metal pole changed to his left hand. This time he struck the rails opposite the cells, creating a deafening sound. Of course the sirens were activated and lockdown divided the wandering followers from their leader. Somehow lock down was slow to close our cell door. It must have been a malfunction. It was sticking, closing slowly. The man was quick to wedge his bar at our lethargic cell door. He stepped over and entered. He turned to face us.

'You guys English?'

'I am,' replied Peter my cell mate.

'What you in for man?'

'A drugs charge.' The man nodded as if he understood. This seemed of interest to him.

'And you old man?'

I held my breath and felt vulnerable. Yet I did not hesitate to reply. 'From Scotland,' I said trying to keep my voice strong although my heart was racing.

'So Scotty boy, what you in for?'

'Murder,' I said although I felt it sounded too dramatic.

'What's dat you say, ma boy?'

'Murder,' I said louder puffing out my chest.

'That's ma boy. We are all in for murder, not so? But you man. Drugs? You got any onya?'

'Er… no… they seized them when I was arrested and searched me when I got here. Honestly, I have no drugs here.'

'That be so, little white man?' his face changed to an aggressive expression.

'I give you two hours, ma boy to find me some drugs. I'm getting low. An' I don't mean weed. I got plenty of dat.'

Peter's hair seemed to stand up. 'I wouldn't know how to get them,' my cell mate's words were lost in his breath.

The giant came forward and placed an arm lock round his neck. He dragged Peter outside our cell. 'Leave him alone. You're hurting him,' I shouted taking a pace forward.

'Hey Scotty, you keep dat mouth of yours shut. You hear now?'

Peter struggled and gasped to breathe as the grip grew tighter. He was pulled off his feet.

'For God's sake let him go, big man. You are making him breathless,' I shouted again at him.

'Careful Scotty boy, I said you keep your mouth shut tight. You hear me?' he said his eyes bulging and his grip getting tighter.

I froze, tight-lipped looking at him with pleading eyes which spoke louder than words.

By then the armed guards had assessed the situation.

'Let him go, Arnie. Let him go, big man,' came through a loud speaker.

'I no let him go, he ma mule. He get me ma drugs won't ya, ma good little white boy?'

I looked at a pathetic Peter who tried to nod a yes to pacify his assailant.

'One last chance, Arnie. Do as I say. Drop that iron bar and let the man go. You have fair warning. You don't want to be the target for my practice. Let him go, Arnie. Last chance I warn ya,' said the guard pointing his rifle at Arnie.

Peter remained off the ground with his two hands trying to free his vocal chords. His colour was changing from red to blue and his eyes remained as large as bloodshot golf balls.

'He be my baby. He go get ma drugs. Den I be happy and we all go home, sweet home, we all go home.' His melancholic yet melodic cry beckoned him return to his spiritual home. And to that heavenly home he went when the bullet hit his forehead. The blood flowed down over Peter and Arnie's grip was released. Peter stood shaking. Arnie's prostrate body gave one last twitch. Peter returned to our cell. His tongue was frozen to his palette. Not a murmur sounded from him when he lay down in his bed, staining his pillow with Arnie's blood. He shook uncontrollably. I sat beside him and reassured him with a shoulder rubbing warmth which I thought would comfort him. I failed. He had seen death at such close quarters. The experience was catastrophic for us both. Guards removed Arnie's body from the hallway moments later. Then they came to take Peter for a shower and fresh linen was placed on his bed. Before he was returned, the prison doctor gave him a sedative. He slept soundly. I did not ask for one but would have readily accepted medication if I had the opportunity in order to secure sound sleep too.

The report of Arnie's death had already been penned and signed off by two officer witnesses. The ink was already very dry.

6

THE SCRAMBLED EGGS LOOKED PALE.

Only the half tomato added colour to the insipid offering. I was not hungry anyway. I could not wait for the day to get underway. My first real court date.

I took a shower in preparation for my appearance. As I soaped myself and saw the studs of prison sweat fall in bubbles around my feet, I sensed whatever I was being set up for, I'd be clean. My set of clothes was returned to me and I dressed each item like greeting a long lost friend.

It was the same court room I had appeared in so briefly before. I sat awaiting the proceedings to begin.

'Just for the record Jack, you still deny the charge?'

'Yes Dave, most certainly yes.'

I noticed the press gallery had some of its pencil sharp recorders present, no doubt noting it was a foreigner before them that day and of course they had heard it was a murder charge. I did not have to wait long, neither did they.

We stood when Judge Ruddy Stein took his position. He ordered us to be seated by a nod of his head.

'Court of the State of Florida in session. Judge Ruddy Stein presiding,' said the gun belted court official. Another nod got the prosecuting attorney to her feet.

'This is case Number MF3278; the State of Florida against Mr Jack Watson. The State alleges that on the twenty third of February in the Apalachee national Park in Taylor County of the State of Florida, you Jack Watson, along with others unknown, did murder Gary McFaul.'

A moment's silence seemed much longer. Then I was addressed personally.

'Please stand Mr Watson. How do you plead to the indictment of first degree murder?'

I stood up and looked the Judge straight in the eye and shook my head.

'Not guilty ma Lord. It was a set up.'

The Judge smiled at hearing my response.

'It is the first time I have been called a Lord. And Mr Watson I only wished your response to the charge not an explanation at this stage. You are not in Britain now, I remind you. Make good use of your lawyer.'

I nodded to show I understood.

'Now, Mr Watson do you wish a Jury Trial or a Bench Trial?'

I had no idea how they differed. I turned towards Dave who pulled my sleeve and I sat down.

'Leave this to me Jack,' he said before standing. 'My client wishes a Trial Jury.'

'Very well,' said the presiding Judge and the clerk to the Court announced: 'Trial set for September 5th.'

After the Judge left his bench I turned to Dave. 'So why the Jury trial?' I asked for clarification.

'Jack, I want your emotion to be seen, an elderly Scottish man with many doubts about this case. The jury will love you for that. They'll empathise. It's worth taking that risk.'

'And not a Bench trial?'

'No, the Judge is appointed by the State. If too many cases of not guilty come from the Bench trial, then he runs the risk of de-selection. You can't take that risk. You can't second guess his past verdicts. Guilty he'd think, before a word of evidence reaches the Judges ear. No, it's a Jury trial you want my friend, trust me.'

Six weeks hence and that meant back into custody, albeit a remand unit once again. Dave came with me. We returned to the interview room but no coffee was ordered this time. Dave had other cases to attend to and he made that clear.

'Before you go, tell me what happed to Garry McFaul. I've not heard much more than he was murdered. Tell me about the others I was said to be with too.'

'True, I wanted to see if the prosecuting attorney might drop the charge at the last minute. So I'd best come clean with you on that. Yes, I know what happened and it's not a pretty sight. Gary, or Daniel Gary McFaul, as you say, had his genitals cut off; his mouth taped and then was hanged on a tree in Apalachee National Park. I showed the photos to you. Didn't I?'

'Yeah, you did but I didn't see him hang on the tree, I'm sure of that.'

'No, I gave you only a few photos. His body was found on the banks of Lake Lafayette, nearby, just off Route 27.'

'Now that I remember, the lake, in the photos.'

Surprises always challenged me. I don't like them. They catch me off balance. This surprise was no different. I tried to imagine the scene. It was indeed gruesome.

'God almighty. And do you possibly think I did all that, I mean, kill him in that way?'

'That's at the heart of the case Jack. You've given me a can of worms to sort through.'

'Blinking heck, what a mess,' was all I could utter and Dave stood up and left.

A six week stalemate was to follow. At least compensation for wrongful arrest could be granted and even if in a corrupted world I was found guilty, they would have to take this prison time off my sentence and with, I presume good behaviour, I might be seeing some shorter time in prison. But why think this way? I could also face death yet I had nothing to do with Gary's demise.

At the end of the second week, Dave sent me a letter with a self addressed envelope. I sat down. There was no scope for ifs and buts. He simply wanted responses so I gave them to him.

Question	Response
Earlier this year, were you in America? Yes/No.	Yes, I replied.

Were you in South Carolina?
Yes/No.   Yes

Did you go south to Georgia?
Yes/ No   Yes

Did you attend any
community meetings?
Yes/No   Yes

Did you enter Florida?
Yes/No   No

Do you know the purpose
of the RIVOSO Organisation?
Yes/No   —

Did you donate to
this organisation?
Yes/No   —

The last two questions required further explanation before I could answer. Back in my cell I tried to understand why a sticky web was encroaching and I was not able or even aware how I could avoid its increasing constriction. I had forgotten about RIVOSO and my contribution. What else had I forgotten? The murder? Anyway at least my responses would bring Dave to me and I'd hear how the case was progressing.

Two days after I had posted my reply I was taken to the interview room where Dave was seated. He did not lift his eyes from his papers. I detected a different attitude this morning.

He looked up at me with a frown. 'Why the hell did you not tell me you were in America at the start of this year, Jack?'

I remembered it was indeed in winter, this last winter. I was in America yes, I was, but I had divorced that fact from my current predicament.

'That was four months ago. From what you tell me I was in America when Gary was murdered but I assure you I wasn't in Florida. The two don't add up,' I said in a voice hoping for understanding.

'Christ, the prosecuting Attorney is having a field day with you. You did give money to RIVOSO, didn't you?'

'Well yes, but it wasn't much. A collecting bowl came round and I threw a few notes in. That was all.'

'Do you know what RIVOSO stands for?'

'Well sort of.'

'What sort of answer is that?' Dave shouted at me.

'I was in Georgia at the time, Atlanta in fact staying with my cousin, celebrating New Year. I saw there was a meeting of survivors of abuse in the paper. I was drawn to it, naturally. It was in a community hall downtown. I thought I'd go along and hear what they were saying. That's all.'

'RIVOSO Jack?' he repeated with staring hot eyes.

'Yes, they did mention it but I can't remember what it stands for, I've forgotten. You know I have memory problems,' I said shaking my head.

'Then let me remind you. Revenge Is Victory Over Sexual Offenders. Does R I V O S O, make any sense to you now?'

I could not fault his logic. 'Well, now it does. It's not the way we do it in Scotland,' I found myself saying twiddling my thumbs around each other.

'No, but it's the way it is done here. And you Jack, are now in the thick of it.'

'Really?

'Jack, you really are. Now think carefully. Explain how your hired car was seen at the murder scene?'

'My car?'

'Yes, your hired car 8319 VJ. Caught on CCTV leaving the murder site.

You could have heard a pin drop after my gasp. My limbs tensed. I turned my mind over and over. It came up with no answer. But how could I be involved? It was still a dark tunnel I was hurtling down and it frustrated me as much as Dave.

'Where's all this evidence coming from, Dave. Who's behind all this?'

'The prosecution have been sharing their evidence with me and it don't look good, Jack.'

I was unable to come up with any better defence. I folded my arms in a tight grip.

'Dave, I don't like where this case is going.' That much was true.

'Jack, there's too much circumstantial evidence around. You don't like where it's going? How do you think I feel?'

He stood up and without saying anything left the interview room without a further word. I detected an aloofness, a disappointment with me but my anxiety reached new depths when I realised he had passed the gents toilet and headed towards the final door without as much as a wave or look back. There was something troubling Dave and it just had to be about my case.

All remand prisoners were on edge. Unlike the timers who were resigned to their punishment, those on remand had a burden. They did not know if their defence would stand up. Their heads were full of lying possibilities which might set them free. I heard many of these theories for they often came to me to test out their court connivances. They saw me as the older wiser one who, they had learned through chat, had court work experience in Scotland or perhaps it was simply because I was a stranger, someone with no dirty hands or dubious contacts in the land. I got to know one young lad. Ron Skeene was an electrician who was accused of killing a young colleague at his work. Well, electrocuted to be more accurate. His defence ploy was based on the theory that it was a complete accident at the work place. A stray live wire had come in contact with the deceased. The fact was Nathaniel was dead and he was accused of killing him.

'You seem to have a plausible defence, I said. Work station for an electrician. A tragic accident is possibly your best bet.'

Ron nodded as he sat at the edge of my bed.

'Was there any motive, or not?'

'Jack, my motive is to get back to my wife and two daughters and out of here is the only way.'

I placed my hand on his knee. 'Ron, I hope you do but please give some thought to any possible motive you could have had to kill Nathaniel. The defence will.'

There was a long silence. There was little physical movement but in his eyes I could see a mind ticking away rejecting some thoughts and advancing others.

'Nathaniel owed me money,' he eventually said.

'Much?'

'Yeah, a lot.'

'What are you talking about?'

'$2,000.'

'That's a lot,' I replied, inviting further disclosure.

Ron tightened his lips. 'Yes, a lot. It's what you get for shutting up, hush money.'

I was out of my league. 'What do you mean, Ron?'

'I knew Nathaniel's secret. He knew his parents would be furious if they knew. So he said he'd pay to hush me up.'

Ron did not seem like a vengeful character. In fact I was warming to him. 'So this money deal was behind the murder...or accident?' I added at the last moment.

'That's what the State thinks was my motive.'

'But if your attorney knows about this and does not hide it, it could be less important in the juror's mind, a distraction,' I suggested.

Ron looked up assessing me it seemed. 'Sounds like you really know the law.'

'Well as I told you, once upon I time I prosecuted offending children to have them referred back to children's hearings and took appeals of their cases at court and in their interests. I knew the tricks of the defence solicitors.'

Ron smiled and raised his eyebrows. He was happy to share even more about his situation.

'You won't believe it, me an electrician, but my dad is a State Judge.'

'Hmmm, lucky I'd say.'

'A double edged sword if you ask me. They have to be impartial. More likely they could throw the whole book at me, just to seem fair.'

Ron's trial took place three days later. We went through a farewell valedictory ceremony ending with a fist bumping. That took me by surprise. In a way I'd like to see him again. He was good company but if he won his case I'd never see him again. If he was found guilty, he'd be removed from remand. But would that mean I might eventually join him there? These were anxious days for me as well as him.

My thoughts returned to that hired car. I simply could not imagine how it found its way to Gary's corpse. Unless there was no State boundary and I slipped over perhaps. But I doubted that. I counted the days. I was a week away from my trial.

7

TWO DAYS HAD ELAPSED AND I HAD NEITHER seen Ron nor heard of his court case. The following morning however I received a letter, already opened for security purposes, it was from Ron. He was a free man. His defence had convinced the jury that his employment facilities were an occupational hazard. It was a death by misadventure. No breach of health and safety was mentioned nor was any circumstantial evidence forthcoming. The hush money seemed to be wiped from the slate. The Judge directed that there were insufficient grounds to convict. He wrote two pages accounting for his day in court but between the lines I was sure he was outlining what I would discover when my time came. He ended with a promise to give me support when I appeared. I liked that.

I replaced the letter in its envelope and hid the contents under my pillow. I would sleep that night with his good fortune acting through osmosis into my veins while I slept.

Four days later I was woken at 6 a.m. After a shower I returned to my cell where my outdoor clothes were set in a neat pile. I dressed. As I sat on my bed I hoped

Dave would have cleared his mind and come up with a sound defence of my situation. There was, after all, no reason I could find for the car being in Florida. I had not been in Florida till recently; I did not have the means or ability to kill anyone. Where was the *mens rea*, the intention, and why this *nomen juris*, this *category* of murder? Dave's mind must have been elsewhere as he had been disappointed in me. I knew I had not been his best client. My damn memory contributed to that.

The prison van brought me to court and I was escorted into a holding suite. There were four brightly coloured walls with high windows, barred. I was the only prisoner there.

An hour later, it may have been a little longer, a public defender arrived, his gown following in a billowed trail.

'Jack Watson?' he called. Who was this man?

I stood up. My throat went dry. I simply nodded. He shook my hand in a tight bone-crushing grasp.

'Saul Auerbach, right? You don't want to be found guilty, do you?'

Of course I didn't. That was an obvious statement but who was man? 'My attorney, Dave Felder. Where is he?'

'I'm taking your case. That's all you need to know. Now, as I was saying I'm here to lessen the conviction.'

Lessen the conviction? That assumed guilt!

'But I'm innocent. Haven't you read my case notes?' I asked with sweat breaking out on my forehead.

'Listen Bud, there's enough circumstantial and some hard evidence in your case, I can't run the risk. We've got to plea bargain,' he said returning his unused pen to his jacket pocket.

I felt numb. Plea bargain? That did assume guilt. I was furious. 'That's not your job. I'm innocent and it is for you to convince the jury.'

'You don't understand, do you?' he asked aggressively.

'I know I'm innocent and that's your job to get the message over,' is that not clear enough for you?

He put his hands on his hips.

'I wish it was that easy, Mr. Watson. If I run a trial and you are found guilty then you'll run the risk of Old Sparky ending your life. Is that what you want?'

How had my situation dissolved to this? Tears gathered like the breaching of a dam and I felt the current of the electric chair in my veins.

'You've got to get me out of this Saul.'

'Okay, this is what I'll do. I'll get the Felony category A down to a category B, from murder to manslaughter. That will prevent the death penalty.'

Then Saul got up and left me to consider his advice.

My mind kept returning to where I was planting sweet peas not so long ago, with not a care in the world. How sudden I now found myself risking death in the electric chair or a lengthy prison sentence. Surely there were attorneys who cared for their clients and not thought of as commodities to be passed on as quickly as possible so that the next customer can be prepared.

Why did Saul suddenly appear without an adequate explanation about Dave? I felt my world collapsing. I was hardly prepared when I was called into the dock.

I first noticed all the eyes of the Jury look at me as I came through the wooden paneled door. That was expected. What did this murderer look like? I smiled uncomfortably back at them. They could see me at last. Some of them were half my age and others black. I hardly ever saw a black person back home. The Jury may have been representative of Florida but certainly not my part of town back home. Saul stood up and beckoned me to sit beside him. Before I sat down I saw a woman sitting immediately behind the prosecutor's table. It dawned on me immediately that this had to be Sal, Gary's wife. I caught her eye and she turned away. I then joined Saul at his table.

'Now Jack. Not a word. Let me do all the talking. I've had a word with the prosecutor. She accepts our plea.'

I had no energy left to repeat my mantra but I gave it one last go.

'Saul, I'm an innocent man. I never killed Gary or anyone.' I said it just loud enough for Sal to have heard.

There was impatience in Saul's answer. 'Jack, believe me, I am preventing you facing the chair.'

He had a point. I also realized I mustn't aggravate the Judge. The moment came.

'All rise, County Court of Tallahassee in session, Judge Nathaniel Baker presiding.'

First to her feet was the prosecutor. She was a woman in her mid forties with heavy makeup showing the cherry lips of passion with which she approached her job. She was blonde and her half smile towards me was not that of a temptress but that of someone who would be enjoying a coffee back at her desk within a few minutes.

'It is my understanding that there has been a development in this case. The accused is willing to agree to the lesser charge of manslaughter. Judge, the State accepts this lesser charge consequently I invite you to stand down the Jury with my grateful thanks and proceed to the verdict.'

'Very well, madam Prosecutor. Mr. Auerbach?'

Saul got to his feet, tapping his pen on the back of his left hand. How best could he represent me now I wondered?

'I agree with the statement of the Prosecutor.' Then he sat down beside me. I was disappointed.

'Mr. Watson, please stand.'

I stood as I was told, holding on to the table with both thumbs.

'You are a convicted felon and now you will be sentenced. Do you understand?'

I wanted to shake my head but once more I was aware of the powers of the Judge and I wished to show a humble contrite face. I said yes, in no more than a hush.

'The taking of a life no matter how much you took part in this murder, is a most serious offence. You will serve a sentence of twenty years imprisonment.'

My mouth opened but my tongue was frozen. Had I heard right? Twenty years? I'd be eighty five before I was released if not dead by then. This was a life sentence, not twenty years.

I saw Sal McFaul glance over at me. It seemed to be a face of disappointment. Perhaps she was hoping for a trial to prolong my agony and the death penalty at its conclusion but she did not get that pleasure. The pleasure was not mine either. I turned to Saul.

'How do I appeal?'

'Not yet, Jack. Let's let the dust settle first.'

What kind of answer was that? I was tempted to ask what dust? He had hardly raised a defense. But one question I had to ask again.

'Tell me Saul. Why was Dave not here?'

Saul took in a deep breath then turned towards me.

'Because Jack, Dave is appearing in another court.'

I looked into the gallery and saw Ron. He shrugged his shoulders and opened the palm of his hands. He shook his head and then stood up, turned and left.

Gone was Ron and gone was Dave who could not represent me anymore. He had thrown in the towel. There were too many doubts in his mind. But I hadn't. I needed to build an appeal carefully.

The prison guards reappeared and handcuffed me. I was on the way back to custody when I wondered what Saul had meant. It was ambiguous. Sure as an attorney he would have other cases in other courts but, why not with me in my court, on such an auspicious day? Perhaps his court appearance elsewhere was not just the court, but in the dock perhaps? I did not have that thought for long. My mind was clearly wandering. That would have been preposterous.

8

IT WAS BACK TO PRISON BUT THIS TIME NOT on remand. This was the big league with the deepest of tangerine orange jump suits worn by felony convicts. I had to get used to it. The older prisoners, of which I was one, were separated from the young criminals. That was a relief as some of them looked to have been born evil, while others were glaikit as we say in Scotland for someone foolish, thoughtless, careless or with a vacant expression. There were many of them of all colours.

I soon got to know that blue attire was for the sexual offenders. They were kept apart from other inmates. There was still a hard anti homosexual air about the prison. The guards could not take any risks with them, especially as some of their own kind had come out over recent times.

My new prison mate was Fred Selsnick. He had killed his wife after a heated argument. He too did not have a trial for the same reason. He escaped the chair. We had something in common. Of course we were both widowers, but under very different circumstances.

We played draughts daily. Chess was not in Fred's skill set. Cards were also a time waster. We were not given chores in the kitchens as the Courts had proved we had all used violence in the past and knives were not seen as compatible with our stay. I understood their reasoning. There was no point either in painting half rooms, then waiting till they dried, scraping them down and re-painting over and over again to make excellent painters on release. Our working days were over and so I chose to work in the library. Much to my surprise several of my books were there already.

So the routine, the first few days of a life sentence, got underway. One I had to accept. Then one day I noticed on a notice board, names were being sought for interest in the Prison Visiting scheme. I put my name down. It would mean a Friday weekly visit from the well meaning community specifically speaking to those whose family may have been miles away in another State. That made me a prime target for their interest as I had come from Europe. Indeed as a Scot, that seemed to go down well. They would all know something of our Nessie, Caber tossing, bagpipes and funny accents, and not to mention our mad keen soccer which was gaining support all over the States. I would see it as contact from the outside world, the world of the non-offending community, from which I had ever so easily slipped.

Larry Hanson was selected as my weekly contact. He was a large man I reckoned some ten years younger than me. He was standing when I entered the hall. I was directed to him and he stretched out his welcoming hand.

'Hi I'm Larry. Good to meet you,' he said with a generous smile.

'I guess you know I'm Jack Watson from Scotland.'

'Yea, they told me that.'

We sat down with a table between us at knee height. It meant we could not get too close to one another.

'So what made you want to do prison visitation?' I asked out of curiosity.

'Well Jack, I served my time as a police officer. Deputy Chief I was. So I'm showing I do not hold a grudge with the criminals I dealt with. I was an honest cop who charged the guilty, warned the feckless and reprimanded with cautions whenever I could. There's lots of police who are good men and women. Only a few are bad apples.'

'I agree,' I nodded. 'I've not met many who were bad. But there again I have not met many at all.'

The first meeting led to my account from the sweet pea planting to my present circumstances. By the time I had finished, it was almost time for him to leave.

'So that's me. What about you? Are you allowed to give any secrets away?'

The bell rang. Chairs were returned to their tables and prisoners stood in line awaiting their passage back to their cells. It was where I was making for but not before Larry spoke.

'Well Jack, I'm an identical twin. Now that's something, isn't it?'

I smiled. We had had a good first session.

I woke up the next morning tired. I felt I had not slept all night. There was a niggle on my mind. It centered on Larry's last words to me. It rekindled my memory bringing Atlanta to the fore. Who had I handed out my author's cards to at that meeting in Atlanta? Possibly all of them for I wanted them to see I was an author and I might have got some sales to boost my pension, but there was also a couple of lads, who were identical twins. They were red-necks I was told, country lads from Maine. What were their names? In the recesses of my mind I knew I had heard their names. They spoke to me at length I remembered. They told me their grandmother had died at Dothan, Alabama and their car required a new suspension bracket. They'd never get their car on the road in time. I felt for them. They were anxious to attend the funeral and I knew it meant a lot to them. I could only think of one solution. I offered my hired car. They tried to say no but it was an answer to their prayers. One of them gave me a wodge of notes for my generosity. That much I remembered. A spark was needed to remind me of their names. They were identical in every way. Ubiquitous jeans of course but their tops were both emblazoned with the logo RIVOSO. I could not understand why they had slipped my mind. I drove them to my cousin's house that night where I gave them the keys. They would park back on my cousin's drive in forty eight hours. We agreed. And they did, after their grandmother was buried in Alabama.

Did their surname start with the letter A? I thought of many A surnames. I continued through the alphabet. I gave up as lunchtime approached. I had reached H. It had been a lonely mind-absorbing exercise. I had the time. I needed a break too. I enjoyed my afternoon break at the library too.

Prisoners reading materials fascinated me. Large coloured illustrated books were popular with the semi-literate. The more erudite sought out the classics which they had always promised themselves they would read, if they only had time. Science fiction had a good following too. The need for escapism in any form was always of interest to this closed community. It was a fairly mindless job replacing books in their categories. The movement of the wheeled trolley on linoleum flooring had a calming effect. It was relaxing to use. Silence was no longer demanded in the modern library. Yet this prison library was perhaps the quietest environment I had experienced in any of the American penal establishments I had recently encountered.

I was placing the paranormal science fiction books back, reading the spines and occasionally the back page blurb, it made time go more quickly. I hesitated. I held on to this book. This genre had never interested me until I picked up The Metal Emperor. I had never heard of it or its author but this Raymond A Palmer book had solved my problem. Palmer. That was the surname of the Palmer twins. With that information securely remembered. I felt I was beginning to form the basis of an appeal against my conviction perhaps.

It would not be just what I thought. I'd need a lawyer who believed in me, out here in this swamp heat of a Floridian prison, I simply did not know how to pull the right strings, bend the right ears or collar the right man.

I shared my thoughts with Fred as we sat at the end of our beds that evening, chasing away cockroach visitors.

'So these guys, the Palmers, if they came from Maine how come they were in Georgia?'

'Fred, I am not sure how this Rivoso organization is run. I think they said they were on their way to their grandmother's funeral in Alabama and stopped in Georgia at Atlanta. Like me, they must have seen this notification, this evening meeting. I guess all I know is that the Palmers must have been victims of abuse too.' I stood up and stretched holding the bars. I flexed my thigh muscles.

'You think they were just down to attend to their grandmother's funeral?'

That question took my mind into a new stratosphere. I wondered if there could possibly be a link between Gary and those twins.

'Hey Jack, you think they were down for revenge?' he said sitting on his hard bed.

I let go of the bars. I turned round. I walked over to Fred. I clapped him hard on his shoulder.

'I feel I'm onto something,' I told him and punched my fist into the palm of my other hand.

9

THERE IS AT LEAST ONE PRISON TRUTH.

Despite the daily routine, no two days were ever the same. One morning I stood on the only chair we shared in our cell. I looked down on the yard in which we had our exercise. For those in our more senior years, that was a gentle rectangular walk around the buildings' internal perimeters. Neither of us spent any time looking outside except occasionally to gauge any adverse weather change. Being Florida it meant endless blue skies for days on end until a storm deposited gallons of water and our roof sounded like a battalion of drummers showing off their skills. The temperature dropped, the sky turned dark and the storm would arrive but only for half an hour or so. Then the temperatures began to rise again and the steaming vegetation below rose to meet our nostrils.

I was looking out one morning when the sexual offenders in their blue T-shirts were being exercised. Then suddenly beyond doubt, I recognized one man. I studied him carefully. I was not mistaken.

'God, it's him,' I shouted in disbelief.

'Who Jack?' asked Fred turning round to catch my drift.

'Well I never. It's Dave Felder,' I said giving each word a moment of its own.

'Dave who?'

'God, yes. Dave Felder my defense attorney. A sexual offender. Bugger me; I can hardly believe it, Dave Felder.'

'But if he was defending you, knowing he had committed a sex crime, well...?' asked Fred floating his idea. It was a question which focused my mind for a moment. It was a good one to point out perhaps. But I was thinking differently.

'Perhaps he was in the dock on my day in court. That would explain why he could not represent me,' was all I could suggest. For what reason, I had no idea. But it took me the rest of the day to come to terms with Dave Felder's demise and now his presence in prison with me again but this time in a different role.

I was really pleased to see Larry at the next prison visitation on Friday afternoon. I was anxious to have my thoughts shared but sensitive enough to bring up the subject gently. If I was too eager, I might put him off and he'd find another prisoner.

'It's good to see you Larry,' I said.

'You too, Jack. So, how have you bin?'

I hesitated. He noted the lacuna.

'Been a tough week?'

'No, not tough Larry. I guess every prisoner says they are innocent of the crime they committed but were found guilty. I've heard it myself.'

Larry gently nodded as if he half expected it said of me too.

'I have always maintained my innocence in this murder. You know, when it happened, I was enjoying my last day in Atlanta. Brought over here three months later and I was given a defense attorney. Now I find him in a blue T-shirt inside like me, a convicted felon. Strange that don't you think?'

Larry said nothing but crossed his legs and rested his chin in his cupped hands. He was concentrating. I was sure he was interested in my disclosures.

'But Larry, it was you who got this ball rolling.'

'Me?' he said raising his head.

'Yes, that last minute response last Friday when you told me you were an identical twin.'

Larry smiled, probably because I had remembered what he had said. He still looked interested, so I continued.

'The Palmer twins. Identical that pair were…'

'Identical, like me and my brother?'

'Yup Larry. Was your brother a police officer too?' I asked out of interest.

Larry smiled. I thought for a moment I had got it right. I was in fact way out.

'Paul? No, he went into the ministry. Baptist minister, he's still preaching in southern Florida.'

'Perhaps he should be here saving lost souls.'

'I'm sure his prayers are for prisoners too. But time is against us Jack. You were saying?'

'Right yes, the Palmer twins. They were at the meeting in Atlanta I attended. They were not local. They were from Maine. Now I think that's a long way from here.'

'It sure is.'

'Yes, but they might have had a motive.'

'A motive?'

'Yes, a motive to kill Gary McFaul, the man I was found guilty of murdering.'

Larry leant back assessing what I had said. I saw the creases above his nose. 'You sure?' he asked with a creased forehead too.

'Well exploring is what I call it. Before Gary retired to Florida, he taught in a boy's boarding school in New England, Massachusetts. Now that's not far from Maine.'

I let that fact float around. I was pleased when Larry spoke.

'You may be on to something here, Jack.'

I was keen to press on. 'The other fact is I gave the twins my hired car, my card too. One of them was found near the body of Gary McFaul. That was part of the circumstantial evidence which sealed my fate.'

Larry thought for a moment. His eyes gave away a question coming to the fore. 'Your car, they took it? Surely the prosecution will have a note of the car's mileage? That could clear you, you know?'

The thought gave me hope for a moment. My travels around Georgia would have mounted up a bit but Florida was that bit further away. Milometer evidence seemed dubious at best to me especially as such evidence had not been shared with Mr. Auerbach, or had it?

'Did they take a DNA sample?'

'DNA from me? No, why?'

'No, not you. The card would provide some DNA. Not sure why they did not follow that one through.

Unless, of course, they thought the murderer was a hired man from out of town. They would not find him on their radar.'

'But my DNA would be on the car too,' I said.

'Yes of course but there would be some other DNA not from your hand. You've got me thinking my man. I can still use some good contacts in the police. I'll do some background work.'

'Really? Will you be allowed to?'

Larry leant back with his arms folded behind his head. 'Yea, why not? I haven't lost my detective instincts and I am a member of the public, seeking out the truth. I can share it with my former colleagues.'

'That would be great. It puts my mind at ease that I've shared my thoughts with you.'

The bell sounded a minute later.

'Doesn't time fly by so quickly, Jack?' he asked uncrossing his legs.

'Aye, tempus fugit. I can't wait till next Friday,' I said standing up and turning towards the line of inmates awaiting their return to their cells.

The following Monday I was in the library. I took out an atlas and opened it out on a table in the sun. I was in no rush. I leafed through the continents stopping at almost each page and following the coast lines which I found most interesting. For a while I was absorbed in being everywhere and nowhere as I turned each page. The place I was not at, it seemed was prison. It proved the theory that a good book is not judged by its cover, although it often is, but by its ability to take the reader to a far off place in the mind.

I turned to New England and ran my index finger over the towns.

As I had spent some time seated at this atlas and not active in the library, I was mildly rebuked.

'Jack, the books won't find their shelves on their own,' the prison librarian said.

I could have made fun of the remark, but I didn't.

'I guess I need some time to read the atlas,' I said slowly as if she was ending an educational moment against my will.

Mrs. Martin sat down beside me. 'Tell me, what are you researching?'

'Do you really want to know?' I said looking at her from close proximity.

'Yes, Jack. Tell me.'

'I wanted to see how near Haverhill was from Kittery.'

'That's you in New England. Page 83. Hang on let me get a magnifying glass.'

I strained to see the small print but I knew Gary taught in Haverhill, a boys' boarding school in Massachusetts. And I knew the twins were on the Maine coast mending fishing boats' nets. I had forgotten the town's name they told me they were from but as soon as I saw the coastal area, the Kittery name came back to me as if I heard it only yesterday.

Mrs. Martin came back triumphantly with her magnifying glass. She held it above the Massachusetts – Maine border.

'I make it, 33 miles apart. Is that what you want to know?'

'33 miles by car, how far away?'

'Half an hour or so but I don't think you will be going there for a while,' she said mystified by my enquiry.

'I think I can return to the book trolley now,' I said with an inner glow of satisfaction.

Mrs. Martin closed the atlas and smiled at me. She was a good lady. She had time for me. Little did she know how my planning was underway or what it was about.

10

MY MEMORY SEEMED TO BE COMING BACK FROM time to time. The more I concentrated on my previous spell in the States and thought through where I had been and what I had done, places I had been, names and memories began to come back to me. Perhaps the short term memory problems I had been having had in the last few months migrated into a longer term memory box and it was more accessible.

For I remembered it was Dick and Mario Palmer that were the twins. I scribbled their names down on the small notebook I got from the prison shop. I was paid for the library work but being a non smoker, I had a little more cash than most to purchase in the meagre shop. I usually bought candy to serve my sweet tooth.

Fred was pleased that I was motivated. He said I was a spider and I was making a web. I was not sure how accurate that description was as I had little idea who I could trap at this stage. But I did not tell him.

The following day at 7.30 pm I received an order to report to the main hall. Apparently I had a visitor. I racked my brain to think who would be visiting me mid week. That was usually a family meeting time and family was the one thing I did not have in the States or anywhere else.

I was surprised to see Larry waiting for me. I was excited and gave him the most welcoming of smiles.

'It's not Friday Larry,' I said.

'Neither is it Prison Visitation. This is a family meeting hour, twice as long as the Friday half hour meet and I needed to see you. They let me come.'

Larry took from his pocket, a chocolate nut bar. He handed it to me.

'For me? You had it checked as you came through? Prison visitors are not meant to give inmates anything.'

'Easy Jack. This is family time just now. Look around kids have candy and are eating it and giving their fathers some. They make an allowance for families and friends visiting.'

I broke off a piece and offered it to Larry.

'I can get candy anytime. You have it all.'

'Thanks Larry, thanks,' I said slowly letting the chocolate melt in my mouth.

'Okay Jack, so I contacted the police in Maine. I asked them if they knew the Parker twins and they told me their background. It's pretty sobering stuff.'

I drew my seat nearer and in my mind's eye saw Mario and Dick in Atlanta once more.

'They were both kids in a care home for young boys. They had been in the care sector for the past five years. They knew their roles and were the king pins in the establishment.'

'So why were they in care?'

'Their mother is a drug addict. She was charged with neglecting the boys and received a two year prison sentence. That's when the boys were taken into care.'

'Did they get home when their mother got out of prison? Or perhaps they spent time with their grandmother?'

'No Jack. The prison broke her. She returned to drugs and prostitution. She wasn't fit to care for a dog let alone a child. The grandmother? No mention of her.'

I tried to think about the life the boys had been dealt. 'I see. Then what about the boys' father?'

'What about him? Goodness knows who he is. What's more if their mother knew who he was she'd be hammering him for custody costs, to feed her lifestyle.'

'So the kids got a bad start to life. But I remember they told me they worked at the harbour sorting engines, nets and did general boat repair work.'

'That what they told you?'

I hesitated. I recalled. 'Clear as a bell, yes. Good car mechanics they told me too.'

'Sure they got some general boat work but the next day they'd be collecting shopping trolleys from the store car parks or washing cars at night.'

'At least they knew how to make a living,' I said in their defence.

'Black market I think you call it. No tax paid. That made them the scourges of the town.'

'Lack of parental guidance, I'd say.'

'Yes and a total lack of trust in anyone too. They felt they had been let down in so many ways.'

'Not the impression I got of them. They had a swagger, a confidence and they knew why they had come south. That was to bury Grandma.'

The children in the hall were becoming impatient. They started walking round the room. I ignored them.

'Did the Maine Police tell you anything else?'

Larry smiled and huffed. 'I had to work them hard.'

'How, or do I mean why?'

'Remember you telling me how the Massachusetts police didn't take you seriously back in the day you had just retired?'

'Yeah.'

'Well it seemed when the twins told the police what Gary McFaul had been doing to them, they were not believed, not even interested.'

'You mean there was no evidence of any kind?'

Larry nodded. 'I don't think the police even investigated.'

'Really?' I said my voice ending on a high note.

'It seems they got your case too around the same time and as they took no action on the twins, they brushed your allegations under the carpet as well. Probably thought you were a bit too far away and a bother, so they closed your case.'

'Yea, not a level playing field. Just imagine, the respectable secondary school teacher from Scotland against a couple of truant, disruptive and frequently missing twins, and me, an ocean, indeed a continent away of course. That's corrupt, surely?' I suggested.

'I tell you, the police had little time for them, or you for that matter.'

'So the twins did have a reason to join RIVOSO?'

'Yes, Jack. They found out there was a lively branch in Atlanta and so stopped there, just as you did.'

'Yes, and four days later I left Atlanta airport to fly home.'

'Yeah and by then Gary was dead.'

This was sobering news for me. It made it possible, time wise, for me to have been at the murder spot. 'So what happened next?' I asked biting my bottom lip unconsciously.

'I was given assurances that the twins would be detained. They would be interviewed. They will keep me in the loop.'

I digested the information slowly like the progress of a frog in a snake's mouth. 'There's still another mystery. My lawyer is in here, here in prison. How did he find himself guilty of sex offences?'

'I'll see what the papers reported. You know Sexual Offenders believe two things. One is that they did not commit any offence and the other is that they were just giving love to their victims.'

'Makes them hard to change.'

Larry nodded with his dreamy eyes focussing on his professional past. 'Yes, very hard to change.'

I had been given a prison link officer, a jailer whose purpose was to suss out any grievances or detect any frustrations a prisoner might have and pour water over them as soon as they occurred. It was a controlling method as much as a confidant role they shared. For us oldies such anxieties were low so they gave us the officers who were approaching retirement. My designated prison guard was Officer Ozzie Bean. Oswald he had been born but that association with Kennedy's assassin and his love of Black Sabbath led to him acquiring the Ozzie name and that stuck. It suited him. He had a bushy black moustache which hid any soft smiles and he had tattoos on both arms. Snakes, trees and a woman's face appeared and moved when he did. It wasn't my first topic of conversation.

'That Larry befriender guy has been seeing you a lot,' he said pulling a chair up to me in the library.

'Yea, glad of getting some company,' I said as I looked at his inquisitive eyes.

Ozzie turned his chair around and leant on the back of it. 'The word around is you are planning a defence of your conviction.'

I turned my head round fast, almost twisting my neck. He was prying into my secret world and I terminated the conversation. I stood up and went to stack books waiting for re-shelving. Ozzie followed me.

'All I'm saying is, if you are going to make an appeal, you'll need the right lawyer.'

I turned towards him and looked him straight in the eye. He was not angry. Maybe I had acted prematurely. I had been too sensitive. I put down the book I was holding but not before I gestured with it pointing back to the seat.

'What do you mean the right lawyer?' I asked suspiciously.

'Jack if you pay for the right lawyer, the chances are he'll find a loophole or lay so much doubt on the case that he swings the jury with his persuasive arguments. You pay for it. You usually get the result you want. If you can't pay for it you get the public defender. Sounds grand but that's the Russian gamble. Five bullets in the six chamber gun. Odds stacked against you.'

I nodded acknowledging I had heard and not disagreed with what he said.

'If I produce a good case and I'm thinking I can, then I feed the attorney with the facts. That's what I'll rely on.'

'Jack, you relied on a public defender too much last time.'

'He got me off the death penalty when things looked very black.'

'So that's why you went for a manslaughter agreement right? And got twenty years?'

'Yes, I thought it the better option.'

'Jack most condemned felons in Florida spend twenty years on death row and never sit on ol' sparky.'

Twenty years on death row. Perhaps I should have gone to trial and let my case run that risk. That would have given some chance of release or twenty years of incarceration. 'You mean, I've been sold a pig in a poke then.'

'You sure have.'

'So when I am ready to go with fresh evidence to test my case, who should defend me?'

'I've been here for forty seven years. Yup a long time an' I've seen lots of things. Got a feelin' about the system and who's abusing it and who's got a good case.'

'Ozzie are you telling me there are some good guys out there that would take on my case without pay?'

'It would not be without pay. The State pays in such cases. Just not as much as if they had their own private law firms.'

'You mean they work for the love of the job, the defending of the innocent or down at heel?'

'Yes, their motivation may be social or religious, maybe some of them came from poor Hispanic backgrounds and want to do their clients good.'

'I see,' I said warming to their motivation.

'Mind you some end up in this social advocacy role because they are simply no good at their job. I reckon that guy that took your case in the end, came from that brotherhood.'

'Saul Auerbach? You mean he wasn't up for it?' I asked wondering about the man who persuaded me in my best interests.

'Can't remember when Saul last ran a murder case. He plea bargains, always. That way the client feels he gets a better deal and the prosecuting attorney gets through the cases quicker thanks to him.'

'Well, I hope Larry can bring fresh news on Friday. I've got to prepare my case well.'

'Okay, so keep me in the know. I'll tell you who is best to be your public defender if you need one.'

'Thanks Ozzie. Of course if the guilty party gives a confession, perhaps I'd be released straight away?' I said holding on to a possibility.

'No, it would mean an unsafe prosecution. The Court would have to revisit your case in a better light.'

11

LEVELS OF NOISE VARIED IN PRISON.

Only at night did the decibels decrease significantly but night movement itself was a disruption. Loo visits and night staff circulating generated their own low level noise. I usually slept through that.

It was during the day that levels hit highs. Not a permanent high which I'd have got used to, more peaks of din. When a prolonged noise occurred it was a different matter. It meant something was up. Some disturbance was underway or a humiliating moment for a guard had occurred. We were never sure, at first, what the issue was.

Nothing happens in prison which is hidden. There is always a witness, a blabbermouth, a disclosure or a rumour with legs. The noise I heard that afternoon was different. Word soon got out that an incident had occurred in the kitchen. The wail of the ambulance and the flashing lights of the police car swept into our world that day. During the evidential trail, the prison was in lockdown.

I looked through the bars to the courtyard down below and saw the ambulance men take two stretchers into the wing. Officers had a grave look on their faces. They knew this disturbance would lead to an enquiry to establish how it had happened and how they had dealt with the incident. Word on the wing was that two prisoners had been stabbed fatally.

Sure enough, I saw the two covered stretchers reappear some fifteen minutes later. The two bodies were enveloped in white sheets.

12

FOLLOWING THE INCIDENT, THE PRISON calmed down. Perhaps it was through respect although I doubted that. Every man was in it for himself to make life bearable and in truth, I was no exception.

Above all, what I missed in Florida was clear cut seasons. The season I left was early summer when nests were fully occupied and berries started to swell. The early bedding plants took root. Then came full summer in all its wet glory before the mellow autumn followed – my favourite season. Apples and pears to be harvested while the dahlias offered colour and the dark nights drew in. Here in Florida there was little change in the weather. It lacked variety and I found that tiring and monotonous. If only I could get out of prison, even for a day, I'd feel better.

Ozzie appeared at our cell. My cell mate Fred was out attending a health check so I encouraged him to enter. He did and sat on my bed.

'So how you bin,' he asked by way of a starter.

'Getting a bit frustrated with my case, no developments to report. In fact not much has happened except that incident in the kitchen.'

Ozzie lowered his head a little. 'Yeah, the report is not looking good. It could have been avoided.'

I saw he looked dejected. 'How,' I asked.

'There should never have been knives lying around. There is a protocol after cooking they must be counted and locked away till the next kitchen shift arrives.'

'But they have access to knives when they prepare meals. So you could not be blamed for that. Anyway I thought the kitchen staff were all sex offenders unlikely to use knives as weapons.'

'Yup that much is true,' he managed to say with a nod.

'So what happened?' I had to ask.

Ozzie sat up straight and looked me in the eye.

'Jack, some of us make mistakes in life and some of us are pure evil. This Texas guy was full of himself, a serial sex offender. He got wordy with this guy. No one took much notice; prisoners often let their frustrations go in a volley of words. But this was more than words. There was hate in his voice and the Floridian guy defended himself as best he could. He was verbose out of his league with the Texan. There wasn't a struggle, more a scene described by the others as a slow motion tragedy unfold. Tex took hold of a knife and pointed it at his victim who was thrown a knife by a bystander. They went for each other sinking their knives through their shirts and into their ribs. The ribs did not stop the force or direction of the blades. Life for them was over. The blood flowed like the rivers of Babylon. That's what the prisoners are saying.'

'So, two deaths?'

'Yea, Jack two unnecessary deaths.'

'Both serial sex offenders?' I confirmed.

'No, Eric the Texan was but the other guy Dave, he was a lawyer. He was in for embezzlement.'

'Embezzlement? That's not a sex offence.'

'No Jack, but put a common criminal lawyer in with common criminals and you've got carnage on the agenda. They don't like professionals, especially a lawyer. That's why they gave him protection by letting him serve his sentence with the sex offenders.'

It took no time for me to take in what Ozzie had said. I was in shock as Ozzie could see by my gaping mouth.

'Dave, my Dave Felder, God what an end to a brilliant career.'

Ozzie turned towards me trying to interpret what I had just said.

'You knew Felder?'

I wiped a tear form my eyes with my shirt sleeve. 'Dave Felder was the first friendly face I knew when I arrived in the States. He showed me the ropes, supported my wishes and understood how I had come to be charged with murder. He was my hope in a strange new foreign system I had confronted.'

'I see, so you knew him well?' asked Ozzie.

I nodded then shook my head from side to side.

'They say he embezzled his clients over a number of years, so he did.'

I stood up and held on to the cell bars. I turned to Ozzie with a plea, despite what he had just said.

'Could I get to attend his funeral?'

'I'll be honest with you. It's not a usual request. But I'll put in a word for you. You might be the only mourner. Guess his wife has left him. I'd give it a 35% chance you'll attend. No more, probably less.'

'Thanks Ozzie,' I said smiling but withholding any physical touch.

Larry Hanson was there to greet me on Friday at prison visitation time. I told him about Dave Felder of course and every other significant happening since his last visit. There were very few of such gravity or indeed significance to report. However I could not resist telling about Saul Auerbach's legal tactics and Larry agreed.

'Saul has a reputation that's well known. He has certainly saved many from a death warrant but by the same token, he's probably got convicted some very innocent guys. And Jack, I got a feeling that you are one of the latter.'

'Thanks Larry, but it's more than a feeling. I need to convince a Judge that I'm innocent.'

'We're getting there, believe me.'

I looked at the hall clock high up on the wall at the far end. The first ten minutes had flown by.

'Dick and Mario Palmers…'

'The twins?' I interjected.

'Yup, they have been flown down from Maine to Florida.'

'Yes, what for?'

'They will be in custody now. They'll take swabs of DNA from them, your business card and the scene of the killing. Then they'll try to connect them.

'And will they?'

'I don't know Jack. If they do they should have a case against them, a clear motive to kill Gary too.'

'And if they find no grounds to stick?'

'Well Jack, I can't see you leavin' here soon. It's as stark as that. It's a win or lose scenario. No second bests, no second chances,' he said looking down.

'I see, all or nothing. So what's the timescale on all of this?' I asked with a new hope in my eyes.

'That's hard to say. I'll let you know as soon as I hear. I should also say as it's my old home patch, I get the word on the street very quickly from my former colleagues.'

The following Thursday I was called to the Governor's office. I had no idea why and was not told what this was about as I was accompanied to the top floor. I even wondered if this was a preamble before release. I hoped so. It wasn't.

'Come in Mr Watson. Please be seated.'

I did as was expected and smiled as I did so. A prison officer stood by the door, just in case of; well I was not sure what just in case of meant, in my position.

'I hear you knew David Felder quite well.'

'He was my lawyer. First professional I met in the States on my arrival.'

'You got on with him well?'

'He brought me brownies to our meetings. Yes, I liked him, even although in the end he did not conduct my case.'

The governor stroked his shaved chin.

'So you know his wife?'

'Not personally but she knew who I was.'

'I see. How old are you, Mr Watson?'

'I'll be 66 in a month.'

He nodded at the guard. 'Leave granted.'

So I found myself dressed in civvies and more importantly, not handcuffed as I rode out in an unmarked car on Monday morning with a silk black tie drooping from my neck. I was wedged between two close shaven headed guards who I had no doubt had a sprint advantage over myself.

The car brought us to South Adams Street where at 2627 the Richardson Family Funeral Care Home was situated. The building had a glowing orange tiled roof and a line of white limousines sitting along the building. We drove past and entered the communal parking lot.

'Okay Jack. Listen up, these are the rules. We will walk behind you and sit behind you all the way. You can speak to his widow and we won't listen, but I warn you...' As he spoke he revealed a pistol tucked in his belt behind his suit jacket. His colleague nudged me to show he had one too.

For one who died in prison there was a good turnout. Their capacity to forgive him was pleasing and obvious. I felt that too. I walked down the aisle and sat half way down on the left. The organ music was a comfort in its familiarity. Before us lay the coffin draped in flower wreaths with tropical flowers drooping down the side. Considerable care had been taken in its presentation.

His widow Nancy arrived with a brother or brother-in-law and their two fatherless teenage children. They seemed composed like the proverbial swans. Their disappointments, grief and sadness were both controlled and hidden.

The pastor spoke of the academically brilliant Dave and his loving family, mentioning the cases of which he was proud to have defended and were well known in the State due to their notoriety. Only a hint of the violent ending in its punitive surroundings was made. The cleric talked of us all as creatures of sin, no one could claim perfection. Only Christ would forgive.

Then before the final hymn, a prayer during which the coffin was hidden from view as Dan made his way to the incinerator and returned to dust.

I recognised the music of Bob Dylan as his voice sang Forever Young. It was played as the funeral party left to receive us at the front door. I felt it spoke to his era and was appropriate. I doubted if it was the same back home where Bach might have been considered. I stood up and looked behind me as my minders rose too. They were immediately behind me as we took our place in the queue. The line snaked forward at a good pace assuming there would be more time to talk at the reception.

I shook Nancy's hand as she pondered who I might be. 'I'm Jack Watson… I remember your brownies,' I said without commenting on prison.

Nancy took hold of my arm. 'I am truly delighted to meet you Jack. There will be more time at the hotel. You are able to come to the reception?'

I looked behind at the two obvious prison guards. They nodded.

'I look forward to that very much indeed,' I said leaving the next two handshakes to go by without a word.

We did not travel far. The Doubletree Hotel was on the same road down at Number 101. Once more we found a parking spot and the rituals began again.

'Okay Jack, so far so good. Now keep off the alcohol and don't forget our pistols are loaded. Let's stay no more than 30 minutes and then your day's over.'

30 minutes I felt was too short. 'As you have a driver, I permit you both to have a glass of whatever. It's only fair. You guys are too big for an orange juice or a root beer,' I said with an elbow nudge. I saw them look at each other. Perhaps they were amused that I was giving them permission to imbibe.

'Okay, we will. Thoughtful of you Jack.'

I smiled. 'I don't think I'm an orange juice drinker or sarsaparilla man in these circumstances either.'

There was a hesitation. There must have been a rule but it seemed suddenly to have been forgotten. 'Okay Jack, you have one too.'

We entered the Hotel vestibule and saw people were lifting glasses of sherry. We followed suit. At tables were cake stands with different vegetarian quiches on the lower tier, scones and pancakes on the second level with cream meringues, angel cake and other exotic delights on the top tier. But first we invited to the hot table. I turned round.

'Not like today's menu back at base,' I chided as the hot food assaulted my senses.

'Keep moving,' was the instruction I was given.

I filled my plate with a medium rare fillet steak with dauphine potatoes, broccoli cheese and minted carrots covered in a red wine jus. The plate was full but not as mountainous as the officers' plates.

As I turned to decide where I would sit, Nancy approached.

'Jack, follow me. There's a table for us over here.'

We marched off with plates held high to a window table for four. Nancy introduced me to a man almost contemporary with me as Mark Delahey. He took a seat and I joined him sitting beside him. Nancy sat looking out of the window and at what I assumed was a brother opposite. I thought I'd get that confirmed.

'Mark, am I right in thinking you are Nancy's brother or brother-in-law perhaps?'

My question was met with a strained silence. Nancy tapped me on my knee.

'Jack, Dave and I had split up several times before. When Dave was jailed I moved in with Mark. We are an item as it were but it has not gone down well with our families. Many of them are present today.'

'I see. Is that why you got me to fill this table?' I said with raised eyebrows.

'Oh Jack. Am I that obvious?' she asked giving a pat on my shoulder for all to see that she had many friends.

'My apologies, I should not have said that.'

'Not at all. Dave did tell me how keen he was to defend you. That scallywag Auerbach got your case and did you rotten, I heard.'

'Well, maybe but it did keep me alive to fight another day,' I laughed.

'And have you started your fight back?'

'Yes, I think I'm on to something. If it comes off you'll be reading all about it in the papers.'

Nancy lifted her knife and fork and speared the broccoli. She lifted her wine glass. 'That's the fighting spirit I like to hear. Cheers Jack, to your freedom.'

'To my freedom,' I said as Mark gave his support simultaneously in a raised glass.

I spent the next few minutes carving and devouring the steak. Its juices ran around my mouth in delight. I had almost forgotten what good cooking was like.

'Jack, did you see much of Dave when you were in prison?'

'You know I am still in prison?' I asked to clarify my position.

'I can see the guards having a field day. Yup I guess you persuaded them. It seems unusual for prisoners going to a prisoner's funeral.'

'They knew Dave represented me, I was one with no local ties in the community and of course, well I am 66 years old. Not likely to cause a disturbance. Anyway, right now I'm a free man and enjoying the feeling.'

Nancy's lifted her glass at the same time as Jack lowered his.

'You were asking me about Dave in prison. No, the sexual offenders are separated from the hard core murderers like me,' I laughed and Nancy did too.

'He was with them for his own protection. Ironic, wasn't it?'

'Yes, it was,' she said soulfully.

'I heard he was in for embezzlement. That surprised me.'

Nancy topped up my glass of red wine from the carafe. 'It didn't surprise me. I was married to Dave for nearly eighteen years. Our wealth I presumed was largely from his work. When I found out how much he had taken from people's accounts, it was the final straw. You only saw the Alpha male lawyer. It was his extracurricular activities which trapped him in the end.'

'Well, I never knew that, nor did I expect it,' I said replacing my glass on the table.

'Oh yes. It became an obsession. He did so much want to flaunt his wealth. I think he had political ambitions.'

I nodded but was not convinced. 'I had heard it was a joint stabbing,' I said.

'What really happened was Dave snapped over his embezzlement being laughed at by poorer convicts and his kitchen knife was plunged into the teasing Texan's heart. Dave knew the law. That was heading to get a first degree murder charge so he turned the knife on himself. He slit his throat. There was blood everywhere as a result, I was told.'

'Who told you that, may I ask?' as I was not sure why there were two versions of Dave's death.

'Jack, the autopsy showed murder and suicide. They could not keep that away from me, his wife, could they?'

Mark raised his glass. 'Jack, to better times.'

Jack raised his glass, clinked the glasses of both at the table and said, 'Indeed, better times for us all.' They sipped the wine. Jack then placed his hand over Nancy's hand. 'You have been awfully nice to me today.'

Mark and Nancy grinned with a smile at the quaintness of the British tongue.

13

BACK IN MY CELL LATER THAT DAY FRED WAS fascinated to hear how two versions of Dave's death were recorded.

'So why did they cover the truth up, Jack?'

'I can only make one suggestion and that might be way off the mark perhaps. Murder in prison is more acceptable.'

'Yeah?'

'Yes. The public won't turn an eye to hearing a prisoner was murdered. After all they are all murders and that's what they know how to do best. It means one less murderer to be released.'

'I see, you're right. The public don't care,' said Fred.

'That's only half the story. Suicide is a no-no. It is a bad statistic. It implies staff did not see the signs coming. They want to keep that rate as low as possible. The double murder gave them that opportunity.'

'Hummm... I guess you are right. So it was a clever cover up.'

The following day, Ozzie came to check all was well. I took the opportunity to show the word was out. I bypassed any small talk. 'Ozzie, Dave did not die in a joint murder did he?'

'What have you bin hearin' Jack?'

'The autopsy shows he committed suicide.'

Ozzie absorbed what he heard by pouting his lips as his tongue circulated around his mouth. 'Who told you that?' he asked to clarify this new allegation. Its source would be of interest to him.

'His wife told me; that's what the coroner told her.'

Ozzie looked me straight in the eye. 'Don't you be goin' saying these things around here.'

'It shows prison to be corrupt, doesn't it?' I said staring at his face.

Ozzie stood up from my bed and clung onto the cell bars.

'There are a lot of things I don't agree with. Many I can't see why and don't ask. It's about survival. If I raised what you are sayin' I'd be scared. I can't do that. I'd lose my pension rights maybe. I tell you, truth has to be sacrificed.'

I felt like a wasp in a jar, trapped and running out of ideas and air.

'Ozzie there's a lot going wrong in the world. Like me for example an innocent man behind bars. Perhaps I'll write this down for the record sometime.'

'Make it a film. The public like Prison Films, Jack. Make it the Green Road 2 or Shawshank Redemption 2.'

'Yeah perhaps,' I said with little enthusiasm. 'It takes all sorts to be prison officers, as I see it. Those that rock the boat and those who sail in calm waters. Good guys and corrupt ones. Management are torn between representing officers, the public and their political masters. The prisoners, they are the cannon fodder,' I suggested.

'Well, that's enough thinking for me. I'd better get back to the grind.' Ozzie turned and raised his finger to his lips. I nodded reluctantly. There was a system and it went by its rules. Anyway Dave's wife had the truth and that's what mattered.

'Just before you go Ozzie. I want to thank you for arranging my trip to Dave's funeral. I got a sense of a world out there. It's a world I'm ready for, thanks to you.'

It was Friday and that meant one thing more than anything else. Larry Hanson was bound to have news. The day could not come fast enough. Fred knew this was a day I'd return to my cell either elated or in the depths of depression.

I could hear him talk in my mind. He was saying, take my advice Jack. Don't hold your hopes too high. I want you to stick around anyways. What will be, will be or as my mother used to say: if it's for you it wouldn't go past you came to my mind. Sound words yeah, but appropriate? We'd have to see.

After lunch my stomach was in knots. I paced up and down the narrow cell. My mind was outside prison but that left me wondering how, passport-less as I was, could I get back home? Then the moment came for the cell to be opened and I made my way towards the visitors' hall at pace. There to greet me with a broad smile was

Larry. He extended his hand. We shook as we lowered ourselves into our wooden seats.

'Well Larry, any news?'

'Yes, there is. But slowly does it. It doesn't mean you're released yet.'

Gone was my first dream. 'So tell me what's happening?'

Larry bent over. I bent forward. I did not want to miss one word.

'Both Dick and Mario Palmers have been charged with Gary McFaul's murder.'

'What. You can't be serious,' I said sitting back with my mouth agape.

'It's true Jack. Trial has been fixed. Mark your diary 17th October.'

'I might be back home by then surely,' I said in a higher voice than usual, excited by the prospect of release.

'No way Jack for two reasons. Firstly they need a conviction of the twins. If there's no conviction, then you are still the only convicted murderer. Secondly, you can't return to Scotland on 17th October. You are a witness for the prosecution.'

Did that make sense? 'Me, a witness for the prosecution? That's a turn around. But what the hell can I say?'

Larry pointed his finger at me then smacked it on to his palm. He counted two more fingers as he made his points. 'I guess they want you to identify the twins for a start. Tell them where you met and that you gave them your car.'

I leant back. 'Surely that won't be enough evidence to get a conviction?'

'You are right Jack, it won't. They have DNA samples of them now to rely on and they've matched them to the murder scene. That's what will get them convicted.'

I sat back contented. It seemed the last leg of this tortuous saga was coming to an end.

My brows furled. 'What's the date today Larry?'

Larry looked at his silver bracelet watch.

'It's 4: 30 p.m. on Friday 30th September.'

'It's still September? The trial's ages off,' I said disappointed.

Larry stretched over and rubbed my knee.

'It's October tomorrow Jack.'

I smiled.

'Don't touch the prisoners,' shouted a guard at Larry.

Larry lifted both his hands above his head and mouthed the word, 'Sorry.'

'Rules, that's what they are Larry. We live by them here.'

14

COUNTING THE DAYS GOING BY WAS A SLOW process. I was aware on 6th October I became 66 years of age. It wasn't commented on by anyone. Management would have had that information in their files of me but they must have been wasting away in some filing cabinet. I liked the symmetry of 66. Route 66 came to mind. It took me out of the prison as I slept and with the wind in my hair. I took off going west from Chicago.

Two days later the letter came. Of course it was the citation to attend the court of the State of Florida against Dick and his twin brother Mario Palmer for the murder of Gary McFaul. I did not get to keep the citation. I was shown it, signed a return slip agreeing to attend and informing them that I had anticipated no leave arrangements during the trial. Leave arrangement, I laughed. I thought of telling them I had planned a visit to San Francisco to be entertained by the dockside sea lions but of course that part did not refer to my current situation. All I had to do was sit and wait for my escort to the trial.

I was wrong. There was one professional who came to see me. It was the state prosecutor, the attorney leading the case. Miss Sorenson was slim, in her mid thirties, a career woman with heels to compete with the castanets of a Mexican percussion band. Prison flooring was her drum. How the hard surface caused a commotion as she danced from reception to interview room.

'Hi I'm Carla Sorenson and I will be leading the prosecution of Dick and Mario Palmer,' she said as she took a seat by the table. She opened her folder.

I nodded and sat down. 'But if you have evidence that they committed the murder and you know I was never in Florida till recently, then I'm not the murderer,' I said like a mathematician solving a riddle.

'Mr Watson. You are, at present, the only convicted felon of the murder of Gary McFaul. I must proceed on that basis.'

'So lose and I remain in custody; win and I'm set free.'

She lit a cigarette and blew the smoke out over Jack's head. 'You could see it that way, Mr Watson. You realise the stakes are high?' She offered a cigarette. I shook my head.

I thought in silence for a moment. 'Then it's best I guild the lily and ensure I make my case.'

'You will not have to resort to that tactic. I strongly advise against it. You would be found out and that would seal your fate. Now let's get down to business. Why Atlanta. Why were you there?'

'I have a cousin in Atlanta. But first, I had visited my other friend, the singer song writer, David Benrexi, from my Camp Onota days all those years ago. That was in South Carolina. I was there with them for Christmas.

Then I went to Atlanta and stayed with my cousin and his wife to celebrate New Year. I stayed there for the next seven weeks.'

'That was some length of time, wasn't it?' she asked surprised.

'Yes, partly because I am a widower now and as they were both at work I was happy to do some household painting and made a few meals, walked their collie dog every day too, that sort of help. It suited us both. I had a few days free to drive around the State. I made use of my three month visa.'

She crossed her legs and rested her notepad on her lap. 'I see. So how did you know of this RIVOSO meeting?'

'I was not aware of its name; it was a public invitation to attend "a survivors of sexual abuse" meeting I came across. I felt I qualified. I was keen to hear what they were saying over here in America.'

Carla continued to scribble notes at a steady rate. 'And you met, spoke to the twins, both of them?'

'Both of them?' I queried. 'They were identical twins. They never separated from each other's company. Yes I spoke to them and gave them my card. Later they persuaded me to loan them my car. It was for their grandmother's funeral.'

'Yes and do you remember where the funeral took place?'

'Yes, that took place in Dothan, Alabama. That's what they told me. I'm sure I have remembered that correctly.' The interview lasted a full hour and I felt confident at the end that I'd come out in a good light.

We shook hands. 'I suppose we meet again on the court date.'

'That's right Mr Watson. 17th October 10 a.m. You will be there.'

'I certainly intend to,' I replied.

'It's not a question Mr Watson, you will be there.'

I could not relax. How could I? Either I remained in prison for life or I returned to home in Scotland. The stakes could not have been higher.

October 17th duly arrived. The day I had coaxed forward. I was given civvies' clothes once more but not mine. I had an appropriate short sleeved white shirt, grey pants and a tie which sported a few local tropical birds. I wondered if this was in preparation of my release and flight home, a goodwill gesture perhaps from the prison authorities.

I was driven to the rear of the court and led into the waiting room. I was handcuff-free but under close observation by two prison officers. I was approached by a green tabard wearing volunteer. She was chatty.

'Given evidence before?' she asked to my surprise.

'Just a couple of times,' I said as I received the coffee she offered.

'So used to court then?'

'I used to prosecute in Scottish courts. That was before I retired.'

'In Scotland? That's far away. Welcome to Floridian Justice.'

I hesitated. Wasn't justice universal? 'Surely the justice here is no different from anywhere else?'

She looked at me. 'It's what you pay for. Many guilty walk free.'

'And some end up on death row?' I said adding the corollary.

'Only the real bad guys, but it depends.'

I tried to complete her sentence but could not. 'Depends on...?' I urged her to reply.

'Depends on the strength of the evidence, of course.'

I nodded and then sipped the hot coffee. 'That's universal. All cases stand on the quality of evidence.'

'Yes and the quality of mercy too,' she said pouring another coffee.

The years passed by. I remembered primary school and The Merchant of Venice. The long term memory was as sharp as it could be. Heightened by my present circumstances, the Shakespearian words flowed. I silently mouthed:

> "*The quality of mercy is not strained;*
> *It droppeth as the gentle rain from heaven*
> *Upon the place beneath...*

Rain from heaven? No sign of that today. A silence followed. The guards looked at each other. It was the lady behind the urn in the far corner that called out once more.

'Last calls for coffee. Dutch courage it gives you.'

I replied. 'No, I won't need any. Simple evidence, clear and precise that's what I'll give.'

As I was thinking about being able to fly home, my name was called. I stood up and was led through to the court. I took the oath and sat down in the witness box seeing Dick and Mario for the first time since they returned the hired car to me. Mario had started to grow a beard and of course so did Dick. They were dressed in the same T shirts and even their mannerisms seemed identical.

'Please give the court your full name and age.' The prosecution attorney, Miss Sorenson, was primed to perform.

'Jack Watson is my name and I am sixty six years of age.'

'Now tell the court your address.'

I hesitated. I tried to make this less of an issue.

'My address is in Glasgow, Scotland...'

'Mr Watson. I presume you have not crossed the Atlantic this morning,' Judge Ivor Barker said with sarcasm in his voice for I presumed he knew from where I came.

'I came this morning from the State Prison in Tallahassee.'

'I believe you were in America earlier in the year. Is that so?' the prosecutor continued.

'Yes, I came to visit a friend in South Carolina for Christmas and then a relative in Atlanta, Georgia, for New Year and for some time after.'

'How did you know these people?'

'I first met David Benrexi when we were both students working at camp Onota in the Berkshire Hills of Massachusetts. That was in the summer months of 1971 and 1972. He is a good friend and a musician. Hamish is my cousin who works as a civil engineer in Atlanta. They were all pleased to see me.'

'Were any of these people the victims of abuse?'

'Not to my knowledge.'

'Did you ever speak to them about your abuse?'

'No, never.'

'Look around the court this morning. Do you recognise anyone you met on that trip to Atlanta?'

I made a slight show of casting my eyes around the court. 'Yes, I remember meeting Dick and Mario Palmer in Atlanta, at the meeting.'

'Which meeting was that Mr Watson?'

'It was a meeting called for the victims of sexual abuse. RIVOSO was mentioned. I didn't understand what it meant at first.'

'And what does it mean?'

'RIVOSO stands for Revenge Is Victory Over Sexual Offenders.'

Miss Sorenson left that answer to circle around the courtroom.

'Can you point to any of the people here in court today who specifically attended this meeting?'

'Only these two. That's them there, the twins, sitting together,' I said pointing to them and holding my finger for as long as I hoped everyone could see.

'Did you give the twins anything that night?'

'I met many people there. I gave all of them my business card. I also lent my hired car to the twins.'

'That seems a sudden and very kind and thoughtful gesture.'

'Well in retrospect it was quite silly of me as it was hired and I had not named them as drivers of the car. That was a mistake. However their grandmother's funeral was in Alabama and so I felt sorry for them.'

'Did they tell you their grandmother's name or her age, or why she died?'

'No, I can't say they did.'

'Did they show you a photo of their grandmother?'

'No, they didn't. Or I can't remember.'

'When were you reunited with your hired car, Mr Watson?'

'Some forty eight hours later or so. I can't remember exactly when it was returned.'

'Why is that?'

'I think I discovered the car in my cousin's drive in the morning. It must have been dropped off sometime late that previous night or very early morning.'

'And when did you return home to Scotland?'

'That would be two days later on 25th February 2016, yes, that was the date of the flight home.'

'Two days after the murder of Gary McFaul?'

'I believe that is true. Yes, two days after the…' my voice trailed away without completing the obvious statement.

I returned to the witness box two hours later. There to cross examine me was an attorney called Jay Yancey. This was a man whose dress was not quite all together. His hair danced in all directions and his tie was knotted over his shirt collar on one side. It gave him a somewhat comical look but it also disguised a brilliant defence attorney's mind. He put it to good use questioning myself.

'Mr Watson. May I ask if you were abused by Gary McFaul?'

'Yes, I was.'

'Did you not in fact bring proceedings against him when he taught in Massachusetts, some two years ago?'

'I did.'

'And what was that outcome?'

'It led nowhere. I did receive a letter from McFaul's solicitor but it enraged me and I tore it up.'

'McFaul enraged you, Mr Watson, in what way?'

'He implied that we were good friends.'

'And am I to believe that this was not the truth?'

'Exactly,' I said with confidence. 'We lived at the time a short distance away from one another. He never visited my home. I visited his home once and only once and wished I had not done so.'

'So Mr Watson, it would be fair to say you had a grudge against Mr McFaul.'

I hesitated. He was leading me towards the door of murder. 'No, not a grudge, I'd prefer to say a serious dispute.'

'Come come, a bit more than a dispute. Remember you then had a second bite at the cherry. You brought the proceedings again, didn't you?'

'Yes, I did but only on the advice of a clinical psychologist.'

'And why was that necessary other than being an act of revenge?'

'No. McFaul had retired to Florida. I feared his abuse might be continuing.'

'Very laudable. That may have been the case. But where's that evidence? I suggest Mr Watson, it does not exist. You know that sex offenders rarely get over their disgusting habits?'

'I know that to be true.'

'So you had a vested interest in seeing McGraw killed, not so?'

'I wanted McFaul to be brought to justice that was all, no not killed.'

'Oh no Mr Watson, you stayed on in Atlanta to see McFaul murdered. Or you arranged for foot soldiers to attend to your dirty work, not so? Then conveniently you boarded a flight home only some forty eight hours after McFaul had met his untimely end.'

'No, I lent my car to the twins. They had the car during the significant time of the murder.'

'Speculation Mr Watson. The twins were attending their grandmother's funeral in Alabama as you know too well.'

I did not regard that as a question and did not wish to reply. As the moments passed I observed Mr Yancey. He seemed to have come to the end of his notes. I was beginning to sense relief. I was wrong.

'Mr Watson, did you note the milometer reading when you had the vehicle returned?'

'I can't say I did.'

'How convenient. A round trip from Atlanta to Tallahassee is 546 miles. Take it from me Mr Watson, the distance from Atlanta to Dothan and back is 412 miles. I put it to you that it wasn't my grieving clients who were in Tallahassee, but you.'

'That's simply not true.'

'Objection.'

'Miss Sorenson,' said the Judge raising his eyes from his notes.

'My friend is being obtuse. Surely as a prosecutor if I had been able to link Mr Watson's travel to Tallahassee, that evidence would have been added to his murder charge? But it wasn't. My friend is however right to say the two-way distance between Atlanta and Tallahassee is 546 miles. The actual reading was 446, exactly 100 miles short of 546. The discrepancy was caused by a short circuit break in the milometer. I wish that to be placed on record.'

'Mr Yancey?'

'Thank you judge. My friend cannot conclude who tampered with the mileage device and so it's rather a red herring.'

'Objection.'

'Miss Sorenson.'

'It can only be circumstantial evidence but I infer that the two accused have the knowledge and guile of mechanical know-how to alter readings and are more likely to have done so. Mr Watson is a child law expert not a mechanic. Nor would he have the reason to tamper with the mileage. I agree circumstantial evidence, for what it's worth,' she said and promptly sat down with a smile at her adversary.

Mr Yancey pouted his lips and stroked his chin.

'I have just one more question Mr Watson. Where did you come from this morning?'

'From the Tallahassee prison,' I said in a clear voice this time.

'Ah yes, I remember. You are there for the murder of Gary McFaul is that not so?'

Mr Yancey did not look at me for my answer. He looked at the jurors and left them to draw their own conclusions.

I felt gutted. I was not sure how to reply for a moment I considered that I should mention my appeal's progress, but it was too late.

'I have no further questions. Thank you Mr Watson.'

'You may stand down Mr Watson,' said the Judge. Ms Sorenson gestured to me to sit behind her to hear the rest of the case. The prison staff new better than to question her wisdom and if truth be told, it meant a more interesting day for them rather than the drudgery of work at the prison.

First Mario came into the witness box and was sworn in. Miss Sorenson got underway wielding her axe.

'Mr Mario Palmer. First please accept my condolences for the death of your grandmother.'

Mario nodded with grace.

'How old was your grandmother?'

'She was in her 90s.'

'I see 91 or 99?'

Mario hesitated. His eyes looked uncomfortable as they darted around the court. 'Not sure.'

'Hmmm…and the funeral was at…er?

'In Dothan.'

'In Dothan. Is that on the south side of the town or not?'

Mario frowned. It was a question he could not answer until a light was lit in his mind, 'Sat Nav got us there, not sure where it was in the town really,' he said triumphantly with a slight smile.

'Did many attend?'

'No, not many,' he replied with confidence growing in his responses.

'Apart from you and your brother about 10 or 20 or thirty perhaps?'

'Objection. Miss Sorenson is procrastinating. I don't see why my client has to endure such grief over and over again.'

The Judge nodded. Ms Sorensen, come to your point please.'

'I will Judge. I was just setting the scene. What was your grandmother's name Mario?'

Mr Yancey looked at the Judge once again and caught his eye. He gave the prosecutor one more chance.

'Molly Palmer was her name,' came his response.

Miss Sorenson lifted a couple of sheets and offered them to the court as productions.

'These are the names of all the funerals that took place over the whole week in question, in Dothan. Mr Yancey, there is no mention of Molly or any other Palmer in any of them. Granny Palmer did not die. She did not exist.' Miss Sorenson handed the papers over to Mr Yancey.

'Mario I put it to you that you were never in Alabama and did not attend your grandmother's funeral but in that crucial forty eight hour window you drove to Florida with one aim in mind, to kill Gary McFaul. Is that not the case?'

Miss Sorenson let the moment linger. 'And who altered the milometer, was it you or your brother?'

Mario froze. He looked down at his feet. The moment was not lost as Miss Sorenson turned to look at the jurors. Mario had no way to dispute the prosecutor's evidence, and was visibly relieved to have been stood down.

The next witness was from police officer Dan Hewlett. His evidence showed my DNA in the hired car as well as the twins of course. My business card was also found at the scene of the murder. That did not alarm me anymore. However the twins DNAs and fingerprints were on the mouth plaster to restrain Gary's painful cries.

From thereon it grew darker and darker for the twins. Towards the end of the day, the jury were sent to retire for their determination of the case.

I thought it might be a quick decision. I hoped it would be thorough too, for my freedom was at stake. One thing made clear to me was I would be driven back to the court to hear the verdict when it came. I was in the eyes of the law still a convicted murderer who had given his evidence and that was that.

15

THE TALLAHASSEE DEMOCRAT WAS FOLDED UNDER OZZIE'S ARM when he called to see me in my cell, two days after I had been at court.

'You heard the news yet?' he asked.

'The verdict you mean?' I asked with my face lit up.

'I sure do. Both acquitted; free men to roam the land.'

I was instantly depressed. I collapsed back on to my bed and held my head between my hands. This cell for the next 19 years and ten months was now my permanent home. It meant my imprisonment was now non-negotiable. In a moment's silence I tried to comprehend how the evidence had failed. It seemed the twins could not account for their movements and the circumstantial evidence had been my downfall. How wrong could I have been? How wrong were the Jury?

Then Ozzie punched me on my shoulder blade. It knocked me off balance. It hurt too. I frowned at him.

'Ya didn't think I was kiddin for a moment did ya?'

I saw his eyes twinkle and a broad smile showed his manicured teeth. He was laughing at my expense.

'Ozzie you could have killed me with a heart attack. You mean they were both found guilty?' I clarified in surprised expectation.

'Yes, I sure do. They are back next Monday for sentencing.'

We came together in a bear hug. Tears began to fall down my cheeks as I held on to a man who had become one my biggest supporters.

'So what do I do now? I can't just walk out of here, or could I on the strength of the Tallahassee Democrat article?'

Ozzie parted and stood before me hitching up his pants. 'We don't get many cases like this. But the ropes are known, you will have an evidence testing hearing. If that goes well, then it's compensation and a free flight home.'

'I hope they can get me a passport in time for the return trip.'

The brown paper envelope arrived opened, to ensure it was neither an escape plan nor a vehicle to smuggle some cocaine. There was no way I'd tamper with the system now starting to go my way. It was from the Office of the State Prosecutor. The official letter mark caused a temporary flutter in my heart. It was very official. At the bottom I saw a copy had also been sent to the prison Governor. That was a relief.

The letter was brief. It informed me that Miss Sorenson would lead the case for me to be exonerated, freed from custody and given appropriate compensation. The case would be heard in the Judge's office and not the court.

It was my last big hurdle.

The following week, I prepared to meet my fate with a more optimistic outlook. Miss Sorenson greeted me with a broad sun blessed Floridian smile. I accompanied her into the chambers of Judge Arnold R Selvin. Another Judge; one who would not know the baggage my case brought with me. Perhaps that meant a clean sheet for Miss Sorenson to draw my case but there seemed to be a risk too of the establishment upholding a conviction. I was not completely at ease as such thoughts filled my mind. She got to her feet.

'Judge I contend that a miscarriage of justice has taken place. Mr Jack Watson, the Scot sitting before you this morning, was wrongly accused of the murder of Gary McFaul.'

'Wrongly accused, Miss Sorenson? If that's the case then it's a grave mistake in your department's proceedings.'

'I accept that statement Judge Selvin. Perhaps I can explain.'

'Indeed you must,' said the Judge making himself comfortable in his grand candy twisted oak chair.

'The death of Gary McFaul was gruesome beyond belief. The State Police were able to find only two pieces of evidence, Mr Watson's business card near the body and a statement from his widow that Mr Watson led a campaign against Mr McFaul over the last three years.'

'Sounds more than circumstantial evidence, Miss Sorenson,' said the Judge twiddling his pen between his fingers. He looked at me and I was not sure how to act. I think I gave him a rather inane look.

'Mr Watson had in fact visited the States earlier this year. But he never set foot in Florida at any time. In Atlanta he met the Palmer twins, both of whom were found guilty of murdering Mr McFaul last week in this very same court as you will appreciate Judge Selvin.'

'Yes, I read about that case. But I can't see why a visit over Christmas and New Year to friends and family led to a murder later in the year.'

'I agree sir. In the evidence against the twins, the court learned they left Atlanta in Mr Watson's hired car, with his permission.'

'So perhaps Mr Watson organised this trip for the twins,' said the Judge teasing out every possibility.

'No sir, Mr Watson lent the car for the twins to attend their grandmother's funeral.'

'Laudable Mr Watson, very thoughtful,' Judge Selvin said.

'However, their Grandmother, if indeed she ever existed, had not died that week and there was no evidence of her funeral in Dothan, Alabama, or anywhere else in the county,' said Miss Sorenson. I checked all deaths in the State of Alabama.'

'You did?'

'Well, not personally Judge, it was a clerical member of staff who undertook a thorough check.'

'I see. Then what about this Rivoso, Miss Sorenson?'

'Yes RIVOSO, Revenge is Victory Over Sex Offenders.'

'But McFaul's widow, she knew of a campaign against her husband. Was that RIVOSO?' asked the wise Judge.

'No, sir. The campaign Mr Watson was leading was based solely on Justice. Mr Watson had seen a psychiatric consultant who discovered his abuse and why his life changed. He asked that the case be opened up. That was in 2013 and I am afraid to say the police were not proactive in Massachusetts. In 2015 Mr Watson spoke to another consultant psychologist who urged him to re-open the case.'

'And you say after all these years it was just a case of justice?'

'No, not just justice. Mr Watson found out that McFaul had taught in a boys' boarding school on the Massachusetts – Maine border. That is where he had abused the twins. Now he was retired and living in Florida where he might be giving private lessons to supplement his pension. That would place other children at risk. I remind you Mr Watson's life work has revolved around protecting children.'

'I see. Perhaps I can now hear from Mr Watson himself?'

'I have no objection,' said Miss Sorenson turning towards me with a smile of confidence.

I stood up to hear the first question.

'Not necessary Mr. Watson. We are not in court. Please be seated.'

I should have seen Miss Sorenson spoke from a seated position. I should have taken my lesson from her.

'I do not doubt you were abused by Mr McFaul. A particularly nasty man it would seem. But you must have been pleased to hear he had been murdered.'

I had been prepared for such an awkward question but I hoped it would not come out that way. 'There was a brief moment of satisfaction when I learned he was dead, I do not deny that. I suspect that was more to do with marking the end of my search for justice and no more. I had no plan to see him killed and certainly not to have discovered the cruelty his death involved. My aim was for him to be incarcerated. That might have given him time to consider how my life had been changed by his abuse.'

'And you were arrested in Scotland?'

'Yes, to my own disbelief and those responding to an extradition request.'

'And was the request not contested?'

'It was and robustly too, eventually. However it was in a climate of the UK not granting extradition requests to America recently. Autism, dementia, mental health factors and the like all mitigate against the government's wish to have such alleged offenders deported.'

'I see. Yet Mr Watson's detention in Scotland could have been avoided, Miss Sorenson?'

Miss Sorenson did not treat his statement as a question and let the moment conveniently slip by.

Judge Selvin shook his head from side to side. Then his thoughts were gathered together. He began to write with haste. I turned to Miss Sorenson who gently raised her hand then lowered it. I kept quiet. We waited to hear how the Judge saw the case. Moments passed by with indecent lethargy. Finally the pen was put down and the papers gathered in a block. The Judge's eyes now settled on me.

'Mr Watson, I do not think this is the finest hour for our two nations as they tried to resolve a particularly difficult murder. I feel you were not served well by your first lawyer Mr Felder, the late Mr Felder, as he withdrew for obvious reasons at a crucial time in your case. You were further disadvantaged by Saul Auerbach who was more concerned to avoid you facing the death penalty rather than permitting a full legal test of evidence. I make no bones about it, Florida is a fine State sullied by having a non functioning death penalty. It should be abolished. The community might not like to hear me voice that point of view I hold but yours is the classic case where justice and truth does not emerge as the death penalty clouds the debate.'

I nodded in full agreement.

'Mr Watson I exonerate you from any association with the death of Mr Gary McFaul. You are no longer detained.'

'Thank you Judge,' I said bowing my head to show respect and pleasure beaming from my face in a broad smile for his decision. My hands clenched tight. I thumped them on my thighs, beneath the table out of sight. An out of space feeling filled my head. Then I came back to my senses as the case seemed to be continuing.

'Miss Sorenson, do you have a compensation order for me to assess?

'I have one prepared,' she said rising and handing the paper to the Judge. He studied it carefully.

'Yes, I see that to be a fair compensation agreement but Miss Sorenson, Mr Watson has no passport. Your department, which has not shown its true colours in this case, must arrange with the British Embassy to secure a flight ticket and a temporary passport.'

'Yes, we can do that sir.'

'Not can, but will Miss Sorenson. But unless you are hosting Mr Watson at your own home, and I suggest that may not be professionally appropriate, you must find him hotel accommodation, not so? Not bed-sit or B&B if you don't mind. At least four star minimum I suggest.'

'Of course, hotel expenses and meals will be met.'

Judge Selvin smiled as if he was watching a stone dry. He waved his pen like a car window wiper.

'And do you presume over the four or five days pending receipt of his passport, Mr Watson will be expected to watch hotel room television and play solitaire all day? This is Tallahassee. He will need some cash to have a guided tour of the city. And at night, let me see, the local division 3 Tallahassee Draggins play soccer. We're big on that in Florida. They play tomorrow. Would you like to see that, Mr Watson?'

'A game of soccer? Oh yes, please.'

'So let me recap. Compensation to the order of $8,000, free accommodation and all meals, a ticket to the soccer game and some taxi money for Mr Watson to enjoy the delights of the local area. Perhaps the police department can be persuaded to drive Mr Watson to the airport at the right time too. He has been incarcerated too long. He needs to get out, Miss Sorenson.'

'That will be granted,' she said.

Judge Selvin stood up and approached me. He extended his hand. We gave each other a solid handshake.

'I trust over time, you will not hold this unfortunate experience against us.'

I smiled at both of them. 'The one thing that an author needs is plenty of experience. America has given me that.'

'The legal system here has given you a rough ride,' said the Judge.

'But a very satisfying ending, you must agree.'

16

THE FAIRFIELD INN HOTEL SUITED ME
WELL IN what was to be a 10 day stay. The room was
special with a good view, the chef was at the top of his
game and the pool was rarely used when I entered at the
start of the day and most nights.

During the days I ventured to St Mark's national
Wildlife Park and wondered at the splendid plumage of
birds and antics of some animals. There were stunning
views of the sea too and it was a pleasure to walk around.
As I was alone, I'd spoken to the different reptiles and
bears. They looked at me but kept silent. I knew that
feeling.

The Tallahassee car museum had cars and carriages
of a time gone by and times to come. The engineering
inventiveness was there to see in one area and the
sauntering stroll of the horse drawn carriages elsewhere.
I liked them as it made me think of the Wild West I had
read about then seen in 1950s television.

I had two Sundays to myself. On both occasions I
found myself having brunch at the Sunday Morning Jazz
Branch at Lake Ella and Fred Dooley Park. I sat near
the band and clapped appreciatively whether I knew the

piece or not. At a break I was approached by one of the band, Jake, he displayed his name on his sweatshirt and we chatted about music. He learned that the accordion was my instrument.

'Yea, you play it well?'

'I've had a break recently while in the States but I've been playing since I was a young teenager.'

'Come on…' he said dragging me up out of my seat.

'We've got an accordion on stage. Go for it.'

It was an Italian Casali ivory keyed instrument, one of the best. It was old but in pitch perfect tune and its solid Italian hard wood maintained a rich colour. It was a large one with fake diamonds on its bellows into which I struggled to secure the leather straps. The keyboard welcomed my fingers as they ran up and down in a fast arpeggio. I was asked to play some pieces I knew well. I began with The Beer Barrel Polka then the slow Georgia on my Mind. Finally I played Sweet Georgia Brown jazzing it up for fun. That was the green light for the band to strike up.

I improvised and held back on some numbers but when the finale medley included O When the Saints, Hiawatha Rag, September in the Rain and There will be Some Changes Made, I was relaxed and in my element.

When the music was over at 4.30 pm Jake asked me to play again, the following Sunday, and I said I could, though it would be my last appearance. I told him I'd be flying home. He smiled. 'Been good to have had you on board.'

'Great to have played in Tallahassee,' I replied.

'Hey don't forget to take the accordion with you till next week. The bellows need a bit of exercise.'

'You've made my day,' I told him sincerely and shook his hand. That then was why I had my Sunday Morning Jazz Brunch twice.

At the end of my stay, I had received my flight ticket and a temporary passport. I flew home from Tampa after being driven there from Tallahassee by a state police car, this time as their honoured and important guest. Little did the driver know that one of his fellow colleagues had brought me into custody, to the cells, earlier in the year.

As I saw America fall back out of sight, I relaxed. The trauma was definitely over; I was a free and innocent man returning home. The airhostess passed by and sought a drinks order.

'I'll have a gin and tonic, thank you.'

'One G&T sir, coming your way.'

'No, er... make it a double, if I may.'

'No problem,' she replied handing me a packet of roasted cashew nuts.

17

IT WAS GOOD TO BE HOME EVEN ALTHOUGH a mountain of mail and grass as tall as a Labrador's eye met me. The sweet peas had withered, they were past their best. They looked sad as I was too. I had never seen them in full bloom this year. It took several days to get my home back to normal.

As I was undertaking this mammoth task of dusting, cleaning, hoovering, gardening, shopping, cooking, the telephone rang.

'Hello could I speak to Mr Jack Watson?'

'Speaking.'

'My name is Jennifer Leslie. I am the Government secretary to the inquiry concerning sexual abuse in Scotland. We read about your release from prison in America and the compensation you rightly gained. You seem to have much experience of the legal side of sexual abuse, especially as you have been a reporter to the children's hearings. We are seeking victims of historic abuse as you had. It would be a pleasure to hear from you and learn about your childhood experience. We would not require you to recount your case in detail but we think you might have valuable insight for our inquiry.'

'I think I can indeed.'

'Then I'll send you details of where we will meet and a travel warrant for you. I suspect it will be an all day meeting.'

'Thanks Jennifer. I look forward to meeting you.'

'I do too, Mr Watson.'

When Miss Leslie's letter arrived, I cleared my diary for that day, as well as the day itself. I wanted to consider what I could say to inform the inquiry. It had indeed been three years since I began steps to have Gary prosecuted. I had failed but my mind was at rest. He had no more child victims to abuse.

Ten days later I was on my way to Forfar where the meeting was to be held. The venue was not far from the Scottish national dog training centre for the blind. I could hear yelps and barks from time to time and that brought memories back of how Rex comforted me as he instinctively knew something bad had occurred. Dogs are like that. They sit by their dying owners and detect unsuspected cancer in healthy people. Dogs and me are at one.

I was met by Jennifer who greeted me warmly. She explained that there would be a panel of five experts in their respective fields, being a doctor, a teacher, a consultant paediatrician, a senior police officer and a senior social worker. There was no table for them to sit at. They were seated in an arc on comfortable chairs. Mine was no different. The Paediatrician welcomed me then all stood and shook my hand.

The niceties were soon dispensed with as I knew nobody really was interested in my journey to Forfar or the road conditions. I had arrived after all. I was anxious to get the afternoon rolling.

'Mr Watson, we are particularly interested in historical abuse. Does the evidence not diminish over the years?' asked the Police officer.

'You might think so.' I paused a moment. I had a closer look at the groups' faces. They seemed to ooze care and protection but could they understand abuse without suffering? I got underway.

'We remember our first day at primary school, don't we?' I saw heads nod in agreement. 'Your first sports day?' Again some heads nodded. 'Neither memory is particularly bad. Stressful perhaps, but not devastating. My abuse was fortunately not as a child but a young adolescent. It was not a prolonged period of abuse but it had drastic consequences. Let me explain. What's the difference between a bus driver, a train driver, a pilot, a ship's captain and a missionary?' I asked.

They thought it an unusual question, I could see as they stroked chins and looked awkwardly towards the ceiling, then at each other.

'It's not a difficult question. They have something obvious in common.'

'They all travel?' suggested the police officer.

'Getting warm. Of course they do travel but perhaps for some it's not travel but flight. It is something I did as I lived so close to my abuser. I travelled on a later bus or an earlier one. I got off one stop before or after my usual destination. It was the same with underground trains and the blue circle trains in Glasgow. I rarely took the same journey home during a school week. And in the student summer days I flew out to camp America and when I qualified as a social worker I set off to West Africa to work. Flight. It's what victims do, some well, others not quite so well. Flight more often takes a missing child to London. Others end their lives prematurely, a flight to death. Looking back, I am relieved I did not take either of these options. Now I'm not saying all train drivers, pilots and taxi drivers are victims but many find comfort in travel, escaping is what it represents.'

'You have certainly brought up a very valuable point, Mr Watson. Forgive me, I should have asked you before you got started, I hope you have no objection for me to record what you are saying?' asked Jennifer.

'Record as you wish I have no objection. The word has to get out.' I shifted in my seat to make myself more comfortable.

'Isn't evidence extremely difficult to obtain in historic abuse?' asked the social worker.

'What I would really like to stress is that evidence in sexual abuse cases is notoriously difficult to prove. Defence lawyers head for the one source of evidential abuse pointing out it often has an uncorroborated status. And it usually is the case. They rest their argument on simple hearsay in addition. That means we must look more carefully about circumstantial evidence. For the teacher it is the sudden drop in interest or performance in classes. There is the apparent day class dreamer who is planning a safe route home that night. Schools are seeing this evidence from time to time but not investigating it. Appoint school based social workers to take these referrals, I suggest.'

'I meant evidence in historical abuse,' the social worker repeated, uncrossing his legs.

'Historical abuse is more likely to be full of evidence. The response to the offence, the path a victim takes, the environment which has its suspicions and in my case the path of professional work I engaged in. Time may heal but in abuse the healing takes a very long time and sometimes never.'

There followed a moment of silence. It gave me time to think what I'd say next but it was not necessary.

'I think we should have a coffee break. We have thoughts to digest,' said the teacher.

'Digestives to eat,' said the portly policemen. There was a snigger of a laugh.

The group had heard from many organisations, schools, police forces and individuals either as victims or those counselling and caring for victims. Foster parents and relatives had been represented too. I learned this from the break and after a visit to the loo, I was ready to resume.

'Mr Watson, would you care to continue?'

I nodded with a smile and made myself comfortable. My thoughts were in an ordered fashion and keen to be presented.

'We have heard of high fliers suddenly losing that status. They leave school with insufficient qualifications and become painters and decorators while their sister is a dentist, a doctor or a teacher. That disparagement can be a further sign of abuse. The child who excels in sums arithmetic, trigonometry, algebra and all things mathematical with sights on being a city financier, loses his focus and the dream fades. It is inexplicable, or is it?' I saw notes being taken by the police officer at this point. That gave me a shudder until I remembered where I was, I was the subject of his case notes.

'I was fortunate; there was nothing to stop me from going to camp America and then to West Africa. But that may not be as easy now. Many children go missing. I ask you why? Many head for London as I already said and initially it brings relief and comfort in anonymity. They eventually make friends and eke out a living keeping their past to themselves. They meet others who have had similar experiences and in due course a bond develops. Thereafter their lives improve or deteriorate. But neither positive nor negative experience is revealed as to where they have come from. They are free from abuse and that means the world to them.'

'Mr Watson, your professional work involved making decisions on behalf of the victims. Were they all the subjects of abuse?' asked the paediatrician.

I nodded. 'Physical abuse, sexual abuse, emotional abuse, lack of parental care; these were the matters of concern, the so-called care and protection cases. Yet many did well after intervention. Some children were successfully fostered and in cases of maternal alcohol foetal syndrome, the child was very often successfully adopted.'

All seemed to be writing as I spoke. I gave them little time to write. I was in danger of becoming a runaway clockwork train once more.

'My life changed around when I met my wife. I gained confidence in leaps and bounds and then by good fortune, in West Africa I met a lecturer from London University, who learned of my work. It was he who believed I could study for a post graduate degree in London when I returned. And that is where we went the following year. I had at the age of thirty, earned a master's degree. A full decade after it was assumed I would have done so. It was a passport to work. A degree was becoming required to work in the field of child care. And I chose that course of work because of a strong commitment to Justice. That commitment was with me in my quest to bring Gary McFaul to justice but my quest is now over. I think you know what happened to him?'

A show of silent nodding heads meant I need say no more about Gary.

'If there is one matter you think crucial to inform the committee in its work, what would that be?' asked the uniformed Chief Superintendant of police.

It took a moment to think, 'I was a reporter to the children's hearings and to consider cases we had to have an admission of the grounds. That frequently meant taking the case to court, as there had been parental denial of abuse. There I would be pitted against some very bright lawyers keen to show there was no corroboration in my evidence. But there were cases where an abused girl was able to draw a picture of herself as well as the abuser on top of her. That was her unmistakably uncle. And a time when a four year old girl hit a doll against the witness box and shouted out the name of the bad man who did bad things to her.

Not forgetting the teacher who confirmed a boy was not at school for two days following an allegation. Not hard evidence in that case, but crucial circumstantial evidence to be built on. Frequently parents struggle to find any meaningful innocent explanation...the cases go on and on and they all have one thing in common... credible circumstantial evidence. In the most difficult of cases, where the offences occur behind closed doors, locked rooms, open countryside, in barns, in empty train carriages, circumstantial evidence is required to be gathered. Courts must give greater credence to circumstantial evidence, especially if some time has elapsed since the traumatic event. Yes, that is my message.'

'You have given us much to consider Mr Watson. We appreciate the time you have taken to be here and the quality of your report will be crucial in our deliberations. You will have played a large part in the compilation of our report on historical abuse. I thank you.'

'It has been a privilege to speak to this important group,' I said smiling at the assembled members while relaxed knowing that my views had been shared and apparently welcomed.

'One final matter Mr Watson, do you have any objection to be named in the list of contributors?'

I smiled. 'I contributed. So my name can be used.'

It might be assumed that this period of my life had come to an end although it took some time to reach this position and I am still prone to sudden painful flashbacks. Meanwhile it seemed the community wished me to keep the story alive. Rotary clubs, women's guilds, even the law schools of this great city require me as a guest speaker from time to time. Because of this I have decided to write about what happened. It is not a dry sad report. I decided to make it a crime novella. In fact, I have started the first chapter.

Let me share the start with you:

'I WAS IN MY GARDEN ON MY KNEES WHEN I was arrested. I had been planting sweet peas in the last week of April, gambling on the end of winter frosts…

Footnote

In August 2014 Professor Alexis Jay presented her horrifying report into the true scale of child sexual exploitation in Rotherham. The findings made headlines around the world and still do.

The reality is that in every city, town and village across the UK, children are being groomed, and many are being sexually exploited. Worryingly, the scale of the abuse has escalated due to social media, with perpetrators sending messages to thousands of children at a time, hoping to lure the unsuspected.

With the high media profile this crime has generated, you would expect that statutory agencies would know the signs to look for, but they are still failing to protect the vulnerable. Why? Partly because agencies still rarely collaborate sufficiently and share information. Partly because the nature of the crime means both the victims and the perpetrators are 'trained' to hide it. Partly because this is an attitude of it is 'Rotherham's problem and it couldn't happen here' and sadly, because is it expensive and time consuming to investigate, prosecute and prevent.

The seemingly wilful ignorance of the crime by some police and social worker authorities is still unfathomable to me. The fact that, still now, victims have barely received any help or recognition to rebuild their lives is beyond shameful - it is letting people down on a catastrophic scale.

There are positives however. South Yorkshire Police have invested a huge amount in trying to understand the crime and training officers to deal with it. Likewise in Police Scotland and their Female and Child Units, high standards of service and delivery is both noted and welcomed. Progress is nevertheless slow while the crime is still escalating. Rotherham Metropolitan Borough Council (RMBC) has worked hard on awareness campaigns and funding existing charities to offer counselling, but it really is too little, too late. I am pleased that Barnardo's will be working in partnership with RMBC to employ 15 workers to help try and prevent the crime, but how does this help existing victims and survivors?

There are three things that I really think could make a difference:

1. Believe victims.
2. Look for solid circumstantial evidence.
3. Prevent the abuse occurring in the first place, rather than dealing with the outcome of the crime.

Unfortunately, until the statutory agencies recognise these three seemingly common sense positions, child sexual exploitation will continue to escalate. We simply can't allow this to happen.

Meanwhile, when such cases come to court, we hope that the suffering of victims is recognised. This novella associates itself with these facts and was why the book was written.

Epilogue

Mick and Dario Palmer were found guilty of first degree murder in Florida and of a further three murders in New England which came to light. It was Florida's McFaul murder that sealed their fate. Both men remain on death row in Tampa, Florida, pending appeals. It is unlikely that they will be executed but more likely they will never be released. A further charge of tampering with a car's milometer was dropped by the prosecution. It seemed insignificant following their convictions.

In Judiciaries around the world, victim impact statements and restorative justice programmes are increasing and used when appropriate. Victims are beginning to have their day in court and at those meetings. Their healing processes are now starting earlier this way, especially if restorative justice is employed creatively.

Jack Watson returned to his home, spending three weeks in his garden bringing it under control again. He returned to his writing and took possession of a Springer spaniel. His mind is exercised in a more relaxed manner now with three walks a day with the energetic canine Eric and of course, his accordion.

Author's Second Note

The seedier side of life can be read in newspapers and seen in graphic films. The psychological damage of abuse is hidden from society. It is not made public. Years of anguish often follow a serious assault or an abuse case.

The effects of child sexual abuse on the victim(s) can include guilt and self-blame. Flashbacks, nightmares, insomnia, self-esteem issues, sexual dysfunction, chronic pain, addiction and self-injury are among other common problems. Revenge, although not so common, can take many forms.

In the United States, approximately 15% to 25% of women and 5% to 15% of men were sexually abused when they were children. Most sexual abuse offenders are acquainted with their victims; approximately 30% are relatives of the child, most often brothers, fathers, mothers, uncles or cousins; around 60% are other acquaintances such as friends of the family, babysitters, or neighbours; strangers are the offenders in approximately 10% of child sexual abuse cases.

This is the background to this novella. While perpetrators of sexual abuse might receive four or six years' imprisonment, the victim suffers for a life time. The Judiciary and especially the Crown Office in England and the Procurator Fiscal Crown Office in Scotland and the Police and Social Workers all over the world need to be aware of this fact.

Once more I invite you to send your thoughts, be they criticisms or the occasional appreciative comment, to me at: netherholm6@yahoo.com

Spot Checks

B&B or Tepee	Tepee in summer
Public or State School	State school
Republican or Democrat	Democrat
New England or New Orleans	NE for scenery and history: New Orleans for music and sea food.
American football or Rugby	Rugby
New York Bears or Yogi Bear	Yogi Bear
Bagel or Glycaemia Index Roll	Bagel (and lox)
Chowder or Cullen Skink	Cullen Skink
Death Penalty or Life Sentence	Life Sentence
Maine or Florida	Maine in summer; Florida in winter.
Oprah or Opera	Opera

Why the Spot Checks you might ask? It's a barometer of who I am, but also for you to gauge your responses to my questions. I would imagine an American reading this page would not share all my preferences. It's a personal statement for everyone. It also serves to make one of the last contributions to this book fun. After all, it has been a grim read at times.

In Conversation with the Author

This is a highly sensitive novel. Did you intend it to be this way?

Every novelist dwells in his mind. From there the stories emerge. Some are experiences, some are facts gained through different media and in conversation. Yet I feel writers write best when speaking from the heart. In this novella, set in the first person, much is true and much is adapted from reality.

Do you have a clear message for the reader of this novel?

Yes, I do. Sexual abuse may be an incident or a series of incidents to the abuser. Abusers claim they start with a loving intention. Such crimes are a moment of pleasure turned sour. A sentence is completed and life goes on. To the abused, a life can be, and often is changed forever, as it was for me. The message is for defence lawyers and judges throughout the world to consider the damage experienced by the victims of abuse. They must hear more victim impact statements. Victims must tell the whole picture of their experience. Prosecutors must ask victims to state their circumstantial evidence. That emotional damage is life changing and lasts a lifetime, must be accepted. Sentencing should take account of this reality on behalf of the victim. Restorative justice where the victim's voice can be heard should feature more in judicial judgements in these cases too. Of course this should not militate against shorter sentences for sexual offenders.

Did you have any reservations about writing this novel?

Part of my knowledge for this book stemmed from my time as the Regional Reporter to the children's hearings. I started this novel recalling the abused children who had come to my attention as victims. Their futures I determined in my professional life. There were also the female prisoners with whom I worked when I was with them in prison as their writer in residence. Most of them had experienced abuse. Then came my own experiences, my reservations were soon dispelled.

This is a novella, quite a short book. Does that matter?

No. If I made it a much longer book I would be diluting the message. A book should dictate the length it requires, not what the author thinks might sell best because of its length or size. There are a few additional pages, even more than usual in this book. Some also appear in my other novels. In The Spot Check, for example, we gauge our preferences and reveal more than you might imagine of me and of you, the reader.

What will your next book be about?

The Trials of Sally Dunning and *A Clerical Murder* are two novellas I am about to publish in one book. A sort of loyal readers' perk: two books for the price of one. I have also just finished writing *Love Amongst Flanders Trenches*. It is now at the editing phase.

You are now sixty-seven years of age. Will you ever end your writing career?

Why should I? As long as I have ideas in my head and I think they might make good reading, I'll write. The process will be slower perhaps. The mind is able and willing. The fingers are capable and my eyesight is good, in one eye. If I lost sight, then I would stop writing of course. I would concentrate on my music. There are many blind musicians. I first met one on the paddle steamer, the Waverly, playing his violin as the ship sailed down the Clyde to Tighnabruaich. It was a glorious summer and I was a schoolboy. I thought I had found the perfect job. I was on the move with music on the sea. Now isn't that a wonderful image?

Suggested Reading Group Questions

Did the opening line grab your attention?

Did the story get off to a good start?

What kept your interest after the court case?

Do you support the Death Penalty?

Would it make any difference if you were accused of a crime in America or the United Kingdom? Discuss.

How important should circumstantial evidence be?

How does this novella compare with Miller's other works?

Note to Book Groups

Do not hesitate to ask me to your book group. There is no charge. However it would be good if you have read the book you wish me to speak about, or perhaps you wish to hear of my life as an author of twenty-three books in different genres? What inspires me to write? How do I get over writer's block, writer's cramp or back ache? How do I balance being Chair of the local Scottish Association for the Study of Offending, chief shopper and cook, musician and writer into my life? I am sure you might like to add your own questions. By the way, I do appreciate a cup of tea and any travel expenses.

Contact me at netherholm6@yahoo.com

OTHER BOOKS BY THE AUTHOR

The Novels

Operation Oboe

A Scottish widow of a Hamburg doctor becomes a Second World War spy in West Africa.

The Last Shepherd

An arrogant city banker clashes with the rural ways of the Last Shepherd, in south-west Scotland.

Restless Waves

A writer in residence aboard a cruise ship faces daemons on board and onshore.

Miss Martha Douglas

A nurse and seamstress, Martha obtains a Royal position but becomes a suffragette. When released from prison she serves in the trenches where she finds true love.

The Parrot's Tale

The comic tale of an escaped parrot in the Scottish countryside sits alongside the tragedy of a missing girl.

The Crazy Psychologist

Set on Rousay in the Orkney Islands, the childhood difficulties of Dr Angie Lawrence come to light to explain her bizarre treatment programmes while her fragmented family come to terms with their past, placing her marriage in jeopardy.

Biographies

Untied Laces the Autobiography

Jim's Retiring Collection

The illustrated cartoons and musings of a city and then rural Church of Scotland minister gathered and set in biblical context.

Poet's Progeny

A line of descent of Robert Burns maintains his influence over succeeding generations.

7 point 7 on the Richter Scale

The diary of the Camp Manger in the NWFP of the Islamic Republic of Pakistan following the 2005 earthquake. (profits to Muslim Hands for earthquake relief.)

Take The Lead

The quirks of dogs experienced by the author over his life in Scotland, Pakistan and Ghana, together with canine poetry and recording medical advances in their training.

Children's Books

Chaz the Friendly Crocodile

Chaz the Nigerian Crocodile visits a Scottish river to help people keep their towns tidy. Set as a poem, this is a book all parents require to train their growing children.

Lawrence the Lion Seeks Work

No more animals are in the circuses. So what happened when Lawrence the Lion went in search of a new job?

Danny the Spotless Dalmatian

All Dalmatian puppies have no spots at birth. They appear after three weeks. Danny's spots never appeared. Follow him as he searches for spots to make him a real Dalmatian.

Self Help

Have you seen my Ummm... Memory?

A valuable booklet for all whose memories are declining. Student memory tips as well as advice for those more senior moments to get through life.

Ponderings IN LARGE PRINT

Poems and short stories, as it says, in large print.

It's Me Honest It Is.

A short book commissioned by the School of Nursing to record the decades of the elderly and offer them a page for their last requests. It is a valuable aid for family members as well as medical attendants.

Coming in 2018

A RELUCTANT SPY

A Second World War espionage thriller now being auctioned as a major feature film.

A Clerical Murder

This is a controversial novel about different clerics clashing, while trying to reach harmony from entrenched positions.

The Trials of Sally Dunning

Sally is autistic and brain damaged. She is groomed, robbed, defrauded and has her home burgled. But will she be a capable witness when the guilty are brought to justice. Yet Sally becomes a sought-after personality. This is a novella showing that vulnerable adults have inner strengths.

Love in Flanders Trenches

The story of a nurse whose family and the local hospital matron made her flee to London and become a Suffragist before nursing in the trenches of the First World War where romance was found amid the horrors of war. With period photos included.